Jack on the Tracks

Nuggets, Gems, Jewels and more. All 100% Dad tested.

JOKES FOR ALL OCCASIONS

NO BALONEY

SNAPPY ANSWERS

DAD'S LITTLE BOOK OF AWE-SOME BIG HUGE GIANT VAST WISDOM

HOW TO BE A WINNER

KEYS TO SUCCESS

ADVICE FROM AESOP TO ZORRO

CONTAINS all of life's lessons in Dad style!

TIPS ON how to avoid ALL OF LIFE'S pitfalls AND DEAD ENDS.

DAD

I knew Dad had all the answers to every question in the universe. There was no problem he couldn't solve. He was never caught off guard. I knew that moving to Miami with him would be a breeze.

JACK GANTOS

Jack
on the
Tracks

Four Seasons of Fifth Grade

SCHOLASTIC INC.

New York Toronto London Auckland Sydney
Mexico City New Delhi Hong Kong Buenos Aires

ISBN 0-439-38465-6

12 11 10 9 8 7 6 5 4 3 2   2 3 4 5 6 7/0

Printed in the U.S.A.   40

First Scholastic printing, January 2002

Designed by Rebecca A. Smith

For Anne and Mabel

Contents

Jack on the Tracks

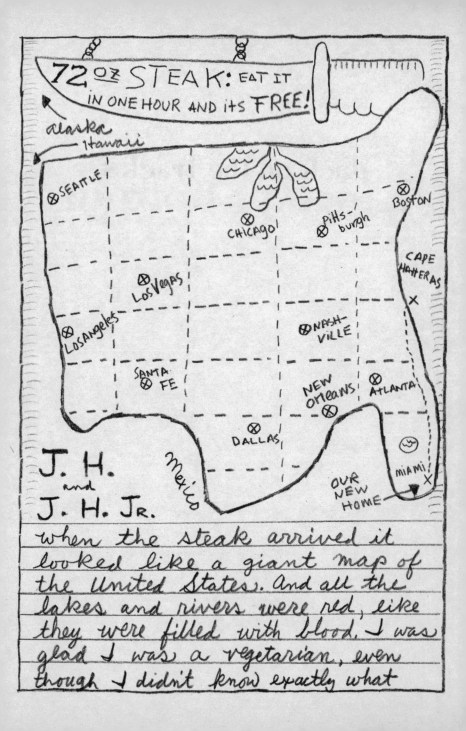

72 OZ STEAK: EAT IT IN ONE HOUR AND it's FREE!

alaska
Hawaii

⊗ SEATTLE

⊗ CHICAGO

Pitts-burgh ⊗

Boston ⊗

CAPE HATTERAS ✕

⊗ Los Vegas

CAPE HATTERAS

LOS ANGELES ⊗

⊗ NASH-VILLE

SANTA FE ⊗

NEW ORLEANS ⊗

ATLANTA ⊗

DALLAS ⊗

Mexico

J. H.
and
J. H. Jr.

OUR NEW HOME

MIAMI ✕

When the steak arrived it looked like a giant map of the United States. And all the lakes and rivers were red, like they were filled with blood. I was glad I was a vegetarian, even though I didn't know exactly what

Riding Shotgun

It was dark. Dad was driving and I was riding shotgun.

We had been heading toward Miami from the moment he locked the front door of our rental house in Cape Hatteras, twisted the brass key off his key ring, stooped down, and slid it back under the door. "That's that," he declared, rubbing his hands together. As he stepped away the screened door banged back against the jamb like a starter's pistol. Dad smiled broadly, then reached into his rear pocket and removed his handkerchief. He flicked it open and waved it above his head.

"Gentlemen," he announced, as if we were at the Indy 500, "start your engines."

A minute later I had a gas-station road map unfolded over my lap and we were crossing the outer-islands bridge, leaving Cape Hatteras behind. I took a deep breath of summer sea air and wondered if the ocean in Miami would have the same sour crab-shell smell as the ocean in North Carolina. I hoped so. When I woke up in the middle of the night the smell of the ocean always made me imagine our house was afloat and lost at sea. In the morning I was always a little disappointed that we hadn't been washed away like the Swiss Family Robinson.

Mom and Betsy and Pete had flown ahead. They were cleaning up our next rental while staying at a motel. Dad and I had loaded up the U-Haul truck during the day and planned to meet them as fast as we could make it down.

"You know, Dad," I said once we left North Carolina and entered South Carolina, "I've been thinking. I have a feeling that I left the water running in the bathroom."

"I'm sure you didn't," he said. "Don't worry about it."

"And"—I hesitated—"I think I may have left the gas burner on in the kitchen."

"I don't think so," he replied, as a line of cars passed us. "I would have smelled it."

"And I think I left my backpack in—"

Dad had heard enough. He jerked his eyes away from the windshield and stared at me for so long we drifted across the white lines into the next lane. "Let me set you straight on the definition of *thinking*," he said, carefully pronouncing every word as if they were to be carved in stone. He wasn't in a good mood to begin with. We had the most powerless U-Haul truck ever built. Each time we climbed a hill we slowed down so much he had to drive in the break-down lane so every car on the east coast could get around us. "*Thinking*," Dad continued, glancing at the road and making an adjustment so we wouldn't cause a pileup, "is when you actually *think* of something you remember doing. Like, if you remember leaving the spigot running in the bathroom—if you actually picture doing it in your mind—then that is *thinking*. But," he stressed, holding up one finger to mark his point as cars screamed past us, "*worrying* is when you can't remember leaving the spigot on. *Worrying* is just *guessing* you left the spigot on. *Guessing* is not *thinking*. And *worrying* and hand-wringing are what nuts do all day long when they are dressed in those little white suits. *Worrying* about every little thing that never happened is what got them put in the loony bin in the first place. So, if I were you, I would really make sure you are very clear about the difference between *thinking* and *worrying*. Because, in the game of life, one will take you to the top of the heap. And one will put you on the bottom. Now *think* about that." He reached over and rapped his knuckles on my head, as if he might wake up the brain cells and set them straight too.

He was right. I knew it, and he definitely knew it. Thinking and guessing were two different things. When I took a spelling test there was a huge difference between knowing the answer and guessing, because when

I guessed I was usually wrong. And around the house, like when Mom asked me where I had left the scissors and I replied, "I think I left them in the living room," that was a guess too, because I usually had no idea what I'd done with them.

But I couldn't break myself from the guessing habit, and as we began to crawl up another hill my mind drifted and I said, "Maybe the truck has a flat tire?"

"*Maybe?*" Dad said harshly as he crushed the gas pedal and stuck his arm out the window to wave drivers around us. "*Maybe* is the same as *guessing*! Did you not learn a thing from what I just said? Did my words of wisdom go in one ear and out the other?"

Suddenly, I felt trapped. Maybe I had riding shotgun all wrong. Instead of me holding the gun like those old stagecoach guards and protecting us from bad guys, Dad had the gun and it was aimed at me. "Sorry," I squeaked, and knew it was time to change the subject before he had me run along outside and help push the truck up the hill.

He had taken a job in Miami selling prestressed concrete beams—whatever those were—and I wondered if he was thinking about his new beginning. I had been thinking a lot about mine and figured it would give us something in common to talk about. But before saying anything, I looked him over to see if I could read his thoughts. He was holding the steering wheel with both hands and staring out through the windshield. The orange glow of the gauges and the sweep of lights from oncoming cars lit up his face, and he carefully steered a little to the left and then a little to the right as if he were a safecracker practicing how to break Florida open like a bank vault and find the "really big money."

"What are you thinking about?" I asked, as we started down a hill and the truck picked up speed.

"I'm starving," he replied. "We left town so fast I forgot to eat dinner."

"Starving for what?" I asked.

"A steak," he said dreamily. "A big juicy steak and a cup of good coffee." He chewed on his lower lip as if he'd bite it off.

"Mom packed some hard-boiled eggs," I said, and reached toward the cooler at my feet.

"Eggs are for eggheads," he said. "Keep your eyes open for a place to stop."

As I stared out at the sparkling green-and-silver road signs and the dark pines behind them, I tried to imagine what Miami was like but couldn't picture anything much besides sharks, water moccasins, alligators, and Key lime pie. I knew a lot more about what I had left behind than about what I was stepping into. Closing the door to our house in Cape Hatteras was the same as reading the last page of a really good book and putting it back on the shelf. Now I had to wonder what awaited me in the sequel. A comedy? A mystery? Or a tragedy? I'd soon find out. I knew this was a time to look on the bright side, but I was still worried. I didn't know if I would make nice new friends. I didn't know what my next school would be like. I didn't know *anything*.

"I'm worried again," I said to Dad. I knew I was asking for trouble, but I couldn't help myself.

He sighed. "You've got to learn to *think positive*," he said. "You know why those two words—*think* and *positive*—go together so well? Because thinking *is* positive. You never hear people say, *worry yourself healthy*. No, they say, *worry yourself sick*. And that is why so many people are sick. They worry too much."

That's so true, I thought. I wished I had my diary. I was always trying to find ways to fill the pages. But I had packed it. "Hey, Dad," I asked. "Will you remember all this stuff so I can write it down later?"

He smiled at me. "How could I forget?" he said. "After all, what I am teaching you are the pillars of truth in life. Once you learn these lessons, you never forget them, and your life is better for it."

Suddenly he pointed up ahead. "Look," he said. "A truck stop. I bet I can get a good steak there."

"Yeah," I said brightly, trying to sound positive as I clapped my hands together. "Great. A truck stop. Boy, that is really great. Lady Luck is on our side tonight."

"Don't overreact," Dad said dryly. "It's a truck stop, not the pearly gates of heaven. When we drive through Georgia I'll explain to you the difference between a *balanced* reaction and an *over*reaction, so you can sound like a smart guy and not a fluff ball. But right now, I just want to eat."

We pulled off at the exit and headed for the glowing sign, which was twice as tall as the trees all around it and so blinding it could probably be seen from the moon. There was a line of freight trucks parked like elephants from head to tail. As we slowly drove by, I felt their diesel engines throb like enormous hearts. Some drivers stood drinking coffee and talking while others crisscrossed the asphalt parking lot, which was shiny with oil stains and crushed cans. For a moment I imagined their lives as they drove all over the country, talking to each other on radios and meeting up at truck stops. I wondered if they had homes or if they lived in their trucks with their wives and kids like the old lady who lived in a shoe.

Dad pulled up to the restaurant side of the station where a red neon sign announced that it was open all night EVERY DAY OF THE YEAR.

"See," Dad said, nodding toward the sign. "Even Santa has to have someplace to eat on Christmas."

"Dad," I whined. "I'm going to be in fifth grade. I know Santa is *fictional*." Sometimes I thought he got me mixed up with my little brother, Pete, who still believed in Santa and Elves and the Easter Bunny and the tooth fairy and bridge trolls. He even believed that when you flushed the toilet in the United States it poured out a hole in China.

"Well, here's one thing that isn't made up," Dad said. "People in the know, know that truckers eat the best food at the best price. You won't get any of that over-priced fancy stuff here that leaves you broke and hungry." He opened his door and came around to my side as I climbed down. "Make sure you lock up," he said. "Otherwise you'll be sitting in the restaurant worrying that you didn't."

"Okay," I said, and felt my face redden. "Okay." He was making me more nervous but I didn't want to show it, because then he would give me a lecture about how nervous people are scatterbrained and a danger to society. I had to watch my step. Every mistake was an opportunity for Dad to launch a lecture.

The windows inside the restaurant were fogged over and the air smelled like boiled cabbage. The walls were covered with old license plates and road signs from all over the country. Dad took a deep breath and rubbed his hands back and forth as he scanned the large room for a seat. When he spotted an open booth, he lurched forward and I followed as we scooted between tables and the backs of chairs filled with big men eating huge, shiny mounds of steaming food.

When we slid into the booth Dad smiled and nodded toward a shot glass full of toothpicks. "That," he said knowingly, "is the mark of a good restaurant."

I took note, and secretly said to myself, I'll write that down too. I loved being alone with Dad. Especially when things were going well, because that's when he taught me all the good stuff he had learned from a lifetime of experience. And even when his lectures got him hot under the collar, it just meant that he cared enough to keep me from being a moron all my life.

"You know, Dad," I said, "I've been thinking about *thinking*. Sometimes thinking is like making stuff up. Like playing the piano or painting. I don't believe thinking is only for spelling and science and math problems."

Dad nodded but he wasn't really interested in the subject of thinking anymore. He was after food. He read over the entire steak section, then he stared out at the other tables to see what the truckers were shoveling down. Then he spotted exactly what he wanted. "Look at that sign," he said, pointing toward the far wall. "That's for me." The sign was in the shape of Texas and read, TAKE A BITE OUT OF TEXAS. EAT A 72 OZ. STEAK IN AN HOUR AND IT'S FREE!

"But if you don't finish it in one hour you have to pay," I said, pointing toward the small print that said the steak was fifty dollars.

Dad was confident. "I'm hungry enough to eat Texas and most of Mexico. So half a cow means nothing to me. Besides, I can kill two birds with one stone. I can get a man-size meal and not pay a cent for it."

"Dad," I pleaded, "the picture of the steak is bigger than you are."

"Bunk and malarkey," he said, waving off my fear with one hand. "They exaggerate the size to scare people. A side of red meat is just what I need."

When the waitress arrived I looked over at Dad. His eyes were bugged out from all the driving, so bugged out, I thought, they were bigger than his stomach. He pointed up at the giant steak sign. "I'll take the challenge," he said. Then he asked, "Is that 72 ounces cooked or uncooked?"

"Uncooked," she replied. "But first you have to put up the fifty bucks. Then, if you finish the meal you get the fifty back. If not, we keep the fifty and you keep the leftovers."

Dad pulled out his wallet, plucked out a fifty-dollar bill that was our gas money, and handed it to the waitress. "Mr. Grant is just visiting," he said. "Mark my words."

The waitress snapped her gum and then with a weary expression across her face replied, "All the big eaters start off talking tall in the saddle, but the steak knocks 'em down to size."

"I'll have it rare," Dad ordered. "Bloody inside."

She gave him a surly look. "That much rare meat looks like roadkill," she remarked. "I can hardly stand to serve it, much less eat it, which I wouldn't because I'm a vegetarian."

Before I knew what I was saying, I blurted out, "I'm a vegetarian too." I'd been thinking about giving up meat ever since I did a book report on Gandhi. Now that I was moving to a new place I thought it would be a good time to make a change.

"Then don't order the *tuna melt*," she said with a sneer, "because a *real* vegetarian doesn't eat fish either."

"Just french fries for me," I said, proud of my new vegetarian status. "With ketchup."

"Only french fries?" Dad asked. "Get the burger plate. It comes with fries."

The waitress gave me a suspicious look. "Are you sure you're a vegetarian? You can't help him eat that steak," she said to me.

"Don't worry," I replied. "I'm a vegetarian. I don't hurt animals."

"Well, I'll be keeping an eye on you anyway," she said. "House rules."

As soon as she turned away she hollered out to the kitchen, "One slab of bloody contest beef on table ten!"

Every trucker in the restaurant turned to stare at us. Dad waved to the crowd as if he was getting ready to be shot out of a cannon. Then he slid out of the booth and began to do deep knee bends. He twisted his head back and forth, cracked his knuckles, and stretched his mouth and lips and teeth way out and around like a horse nibbling sugar cubes.

Then he turned to me and made a face as if he smelled something bad. "Since when have you become a vegetarian?" he asked.

"I started today," I replied. "We're moving to a new place so I thought it was a good time to change my eating habits."

"Well, you can't stop eating meat. You're a growing boy."

"Most of the world is vegetarian," I said.

"Most of the world is starving," he replied. "Think about that."

"You are what you eat," I said to him, repeating what I had read on a bumper sticker.

"No," Dad countered. "You are what you *think*. It's how *smart* you are that counts in this world. And believe me, quoting bumper stickers does not make you look too smart."

I didn't want to argue with him, so I tried to change the subject. "What new things are you looking forward to doing in Miami?" I asked.

"Steady work," he said.

"Is that all?"

"Son, I'm a meat-and-potatoes guy. Nothing fancy for me. You can change all you want. You can be a vegetarian today and a cannibal tomorrow. You can turn colors, speak Swahili, and join a circus. You're young. But for me, the future is all about work."

He spoke so harshly I didn't know how to respond. I thought everyone was like me and believed that moving was a time to make new changes. But I was wrong. The only change Dad was making was to work even harder.

When the steak arrived it was larger than the one on the sign. The waitress pushed it up to the booth on a special cart. She looked like a nurse wheeling in a mutilated patient. The steak came served on a cutting board the size of a piano top. The busboy helped her pick it up and plop it down on our table. "If you finish it," she said, handing Dad a sharp steak knife, "you are allowed to carve your initials into the wood."

I'll be carving his initials on a tombstone, I thought. There was no way he was going to finish eating that meat. And there was no way we were going to get all the way to Miami without that fifty dollars for gas. And there was no way I was going to tell him what was on my mind because he would just tell me to settle down and "stop worrying."

"Watch my tables," the waitress hollered to the busboy as she delivered my fries. Then she pulled up a tall bar stool and sat down. She had a stopwatch around her neck like a track coach. "You ready?" she asked Dad.

"Almost," he replied. "I have to get set up." Quickly he carved the steak into fifty pieces and when he was finished he unfastened his watch and handed it to me. "I'm going to eat a piece per minute," he said. "Keep me on schedule, but if I fall behind I'll have ten minutes to get caught up."

"You bet," I replied, trying to sound positive.

"Okay," he announced, and gave the waitress a nod. Instantly she clicked the button on her stopwatch as

Dad stabbed a piece of meat and chucked it into his mouth. He chewed savagely, as if killing it, then swallowed.

"Thirty seconds," I called out, flashing him the thumbs-up.

"What happens if I eat this in half the time?" Dad asked, and drove another piece into his mouth.

"You die," she said bluntly, staring down at him like a vulture. I was glad she was a vegetarian, otherwise I imagined she would eat him if he keeled over.

I began to think of the fifty pieces as a map of the states. I figured he had just devoured Maine and was now chewing up New Hampshire. He swallowed and began to chomp down on Massachusetts. He was ahead of schedule by the time he ate his way down the east coast and started at the top of the steak again with Vermont. I kept calling out the minutes and Dad kept chewing. By the time he reached Louisiana he was slowing down, and when he swallowed, he began to gag.

"Coffee," he rasped.

"Bring a pot of coffee, and a plunger," the waitress called out to another waitress. Then she turned to Dad. "I forgot to tell you that if you barf, the deal is off. Some guys who come in here are professional barfers and they think they can just eat and barf, eat and barf."

"I get the picture," Dad said, recovering. He set down his fork as he waited for the coffee.

"Take a breather," I said. "You're ahead of schedule by ninety seconds."

After he drank a cup of coffee he picked up the pace again. He was somewhere around Colorado when he began to cough. His face got bright red and he was choking and pounding himself on the chest and when that didn't work he started slapping himself on the back.

Oh my God, I thought. He's dying. I looked up at the waitress. She was using a butter knife to push her cuticles back into place. I looked around the restaurant for the poster of what to do if a person chokes, but the poster wasn't in sight and Dad was turning blue and the veins were popping out across his forehead. Any minute I thought he would pass out and fall from the booth and I'd be begging truckers to help, pleading with them and the mean waitress as he died right in front of me from a hunk of the Rocky Mountains plugging up his throat. I would have to call Mom on the phone and tell her Dad died while eating a monster steak, and we'd all cry because Dad was gone and our new beginning was more like the beginning of the end for us. And all because of a free steak.

"Hey," Dad said, tapping the end of his fork on the table. "No daydreaming. What time is it?"

"Sorry," I yelped. I must not have noticed that he'd gotten the piece swallowed. "Sorry, I was just worried that you'd choke to death." I looked at the watch but couldn't tell the time because both my eyes had teared up.

Dad put New Mexico in his mouth and chewed for a few seconds before he could say, "See what worrying will do to a person—you were paralyzed with fear. Think *positive* for a change. If you expect the worst, the worst happens."

He was right. I always thought negative thoughts. Well, I'd add thinking positive thoughts to my new beginning.

"You can do it!" I said, cheering him on. "You're the boss. After all, how smart can that meat be? It's dead and you're alive."

"Okay," he said, waving his fork at me. "Don't get carried away and start sounding like a fluff ball again."

"Twenty minutes left," the waitress announced. "It's right about this time that most of the big talkers hit the wall. Once a man got so full his belly crushed his kidney and he nearly bled to death."

She is so *negative,* I thought as I cheered Dad on.

He swallowed Idaho and raced through Utah, Nevada, and Arizona, then back up to Washington State. It was as if he'd gotten a second wind, and soon he had polished off Oregon, California, Alaska, and Hawaii.

He swallowed the last bite, wiped his mouth, and looked up at the waitress with a big grin on his face. "I'll have a slice of Key lime pie," he said smoothly. "And a coffee refill."

"I'll be darned," she said, and handed his fifty back. "I never had a little man figured to eat this much steak."

"Never underestimate the power of positive thinking," Dad said to her, then turned and winked at me. He took the steak knife and with a flourish carved J.H. & SON into the cutting board.

On the way out to the car Dad stopped. He took a deep, deep breath and announced to everyone in the parking lot, "Jack Henry Senior is ready to take on the world!" Then he pounded his chest like Tarzan.

"Jack Henry Junior is too!" I yelled, and pounded my chest as a few puzzled truckers looked our way. I was ready. Just watching him eat that steak filled me with faith that he could do anything. And if he could, I could too. We climbed back into the truck and slowly took off for Miami.

"I'll tell you a little something," Dad said after a minute. "Getting a fresh start in life has more to do with the way you *think* than with where you live, or what you eat. If you have an orderly mind, you'll be a winner no matter where you end up. If your mind is a jumble of junk, you'll be a loser. It's as simple as that. You got it?"

"Got it," I replied. And I kept it in my mind all the way to Miami. When we got there, his words were still in me, right where I left them on a back shelf of my brain. And when I unpacked my diary I wrote them all down.

other things
I did put
on the
tracks.

leftover patch
of cat fur
ON COW BELL

IN GOD W
19

1. LINCOLN
penny

2. HOUSE
KEY

3. TOOTHPASTE TUBE

4.
CAN
OF
BEANS

It's true that I put a lot
of things on the tracks.
But no matter what Betsy
says, I did not put the
cat on the tracks. It was
an accident. Tack was there
when it happened and he agrees

Belling the Cat

Every time a train rumbled past the back of our wooden house the floorboards shook and the mouse ran from one side of the living room to the other. I was trying to set the mousetrap Mom had bought, but each time I placed the tiny slice of cheddar cheese on the trigger I clumsily set it off and the thick mouse-killing wire snapped back across my fingers. My fingertips were already swollen and covered with purple blood blisters.

"This is just what I deserve," I muttered as I tried to set the trap again. "I shouldn't kill any living creature. I should only eat nuts and berries and be like Noah and save all animals great and small."

Just then the doorbell rang. It startled me and I jerked my hand. Whack! went the wire down over my finger. "Arghh," I moaned.

"Don't just sit there hurting yourself," my older sister, Betsy, hollered from the kitchen. "Get up and answer the door."

I thought it might be the Welcome Wagon because we had just moved into the neighborhood and a sign down the street read, WELCOME TO MIAMI, FLORIDA— HOME OF THE DADE COUNTY WELCOME WAGON. So I figured since we didn't know one person in Miami, it had to be them.

But when I opened the front door, instead of a smiling lady with a housewarming basket of fruit it was just some squirming kid fighting off a big black-and-white cat that had already fastened itself to his head and clawed him down across the neck and was busy drawing blood from one of his earlobes.

"Get this thing offa me," he shouted desperately, and danced around while grabbing at the cat with his eyes closed so it wouldn't blind him.

I just stood there. I had never seen the kid before. Or the cat.

"Help me!" he screeched as the cat clawed hair from his skull. "The cat's yours, anyway. My grandmother sent it over." He jerked his head at me real quick and the cat snapped forward and did an end-over-end flip off his head and onto mine.

"Arghh!" I yelled as it reached out and raked its claws across my arm.

"Is that the Welcome Wagon?" Mom called from down the hall.

"It's the *welcome cat,*" the kid hollered back.

"What?" she asked.

Just then the cat leapt from my shoulder and in one perfect strike landed on the mouse, which was crossing the room. I could hear a small crunching sound as the cat teeth bit clean through the mouse head.

"That must of hurt," I remarked, and screwed up my face. I really hadn't wanted to kill the mouse.

"See," the kid said, touching his ear. "You could use a cat."

"What's your name?" I asked.

"Tack Smith," he replied. "I live next door and my grandma lives down the street. Do you have a rag so I can wipe this blood off?"

"Yeah, come on in," I said.

Betsy was sitting at the kitchen table reading the newspaper. She was cutting out the weird "human interest" stories and keeping her own Ripley's Believe It or Not! scrapbook. Now, every time Betsy saw something weird she would point at it and shout, "Believe it or not!" Most of the time she was pointing at me.

When she looked up and saw us both bleeding she said in a newscaster's voice, "Believe it or not! Jack Henry had lived in his new neighborhood less than twenty-four hours before he got into a bloodbath with the neighbors."

"Don't listen to her," I said to Tack, and handed him a wet dish rag. "She belongs to a lost tribe of older sisters who eat younger brothers."

"Nice to meet you," Tack said as he wiped blood from his neck.

"Who started it?" Betsy asked.

"What?" I replied.

"The fight," she said. "You're both covered with blood. Who started it?"

"The cat did," Tack said right back.

"What cat?"

"The welcome cat," Tack said. "My grandmother sent it over."

Betsy sniffed. "I'm allergic to cats," she complained. "Take it back."

"Too late," Tack replied. "Grandma gives a cat to everyone who moves into the neighborhood. If you try to give it back, she'll just give you two more."

Just then I heard Mom scream and do a little rat-a-tat tap dance in the living room. "Oh my gosh," she shouted. "I stepped on a dead mouse."

"Believe it or not!" Betsy said in a spooky voice and pointed at me. "An animal killer is loose in the neighborhood."

"The cat killed the mouse," I protested. "It wasn't me. I love animals. Even vermin."

Betsy looked me right in the eyes. "You sound guilty already," she said.

Then she sneezed, and gave me an evil older-sister look that could kill.

Mom named the new cat Miss Kitty. I called her Killer Kitty. She was a bloodthirsty bully who made cat chow out of every creature smaller than she was: mice, birds, frogs, lizards, butterflies. But she didn't eat the roaches. That was too bad, because we had a lot of roaches and Mom made it my job to kill them—although when I captured any big ones I wrote their names with red nail polish down their backs and kept them alive in a big gallon jar in the back of my closet.

One night, not long after we got Miss Kitty, I was lying in bed reading a book of Aesop's fables. Dad had given me the book because it had been his as a kid. "This book belongs in the Life Lessons Hall of Fame," he said. "My dad gave it to me and now I'm giving it to you. It's a classic, good food for the mind." Each fable ended with a special lesson, like "Do not count your chickens before they are hatched." Or "Slow and steady wins the race." Or "Familiarity breeds contempt." I was beginning to see where Dad got some of his lecture ideas.

Each time I turned a page in the book I winced. Miss Kitty had scratched up my fingers so badly they were sore and covered with bloody Band-Aids. But I didn't dare wiggle when I winced because Miss Kitty was asleep across my feet, and the last time I even twitched she clawed me to the bone on one of my toes.

Suddenly, I forgot about the pain. I was reading a fable about how some mice wanted to put a bell around the neck of a cat that had been eating them. They all agreed that belling the cat would be a brilliant idea, only nobody wanted to be the mouse to do it. The lesson of the story was, "Easier said than done."

Well, I'm no mouse, I said to myself, I'm a man. I can do it. I peeked up over the edge of the book. Miss Kitty was purring away with a smile on her face, probably dreaming of mouse pizza. I remembered seeing an old bell in the toolshed out back. I wondered how I might get the bell around her neck. I figured I'd need a suit of armor, or a robot, or maybe there was a way I could hypnotize her. I couldn't think of a plan where she wouldn't slash me to death first, so I turned the light off. I'll sleep on it, I said to myself, and in the morning I'll come up with something brilliant.

I had a good night's sleep and the next morning my brain was working. I went out to the toolshed on the back of the property and found the dented-up copper bell. It was about as big as my fist and just what I needed. It looked like a cowbell but I thought it was pretty odd that there would be cowbells in Florida.

When I rang it in Betsy's ear, she had the answer.

"Believe it or not, Florida is the number-two cattle-raising state in the nation," she said.

"I didn't know that," I said.

"What you do know," she said, "could fit on the head of a pin."

Betsy always made me feel like a moron, but I knew Dad was going to help me change all that. He was helping me organize my mind into a well-oiled machine. I stomped out of the house, and all the way down to the 7-Eleven I kept saying to myself, My plan is brilliant, my plan is dazzling. I was thinking positive, and I wasn't nervous. I bought a flea collar and marched home.

Miss Kitty was spread out across the long hallway rug. She had caught a mockingbird and was busy pulling off its beak. Very quietly, I tiptoed up to the edge of the rug and began to roll it up, and before she knew what happened I had her rolled up with her yowling head sticking out one end and her tail out the other. I sat down on the rolled-up rug and quickly fastened the collar with the big bell around her neck as she hissed at me. "Don't be mad," I said. "I'm just trying to save the animals. Noah probably had to do this with all the cats on the ark. Besides, it will do you good to become a vegetarian like me." Once I had the buckle set I hopped up, unrolled the rug, and struck a karate pose in case she sprang at me. But she didn't. The heavy old bell was like a ball and chain around her neck and she dragged it unhappily across the living room.

Betsy was blowing her nose when Miss Kitty clanked past her feet toward the back door.

"That's cruel," she said, pointing her damp tissue at me.

"No worse than her killing all the birds and mice and everything else in the neighborhood," I replied.

"She won't even be able to get out of the way of a car if she's crossing the street," Betsy said. "Think about it. Use your head."

"I just did," I said proudly.

"Well, you didn't use enough of it," she replied. "Mark my words. That bell is going to be the end for that cat." She sneezed again.

I cleaned up what was left of the bird and went into my room. I opened my diary and wrote, "Solved that problem. Miss Kitty will never sneak up on another animal again. I guarantee it." I figured I'd win the Nobel peace prize for keeping a world war from breaking out between the cats and the rest of the animal kingdom. I taped a feather from the bird onto the page and banged the book closed.

The bell was working. Miss Kitty still wanted to sneak up on birds and mice and lizards but she couldn't catch them. As she lunged forward, the bell clanked and all her victims ran away. When I checked up on her she was slumped over in the middle of the back yard looking depressed after just missing a bloated toad that disappeared in a patch of weeds.

"Don't look so glum," I said to her. "You simply have

to change your diet." I went into the house and opened a can of organic lentil-and-lima-bean cat food I had bought from the sale bin at the pet store. I had to hold my nose when I spooned it into a bowl because it smelled like old garbage.

"You'll love this," I sang as I set the bowl down before her. She wrinkled up her nose, and began to crawl and clank away like an escaped prisoner.

"I'm sorry," I called out, "but this is for your own good." She turned and glowered at me.

Just then Tack Smith came around the side of the house. "How's the killer cat?" he asked.

"She's settled down a bit," I replied.

Tack opened a paper bag and dumped out about twenty small tubes of toothpaste. "Don't tell anyone," he said slyly, "but these are samples that the mailman left in everyone's mailbox and I took them."

"Why?" I asked. I wondered if he was so poor he had to steal toothpaste.

Tack grinned and pointed to the train tracks. "Let's put them on the track," he said, "and when the next train comes by we'll see what happens."

I looked back at the house. Mom would wring my neck if she caught me, but I knew she was busy getting the house in order and sewing new curtains.

"Okay," I said to Tack. "Let's go before the next train comes by."

We ran across the back yard and across a dirt road,

up over a rusty wire fence that had a sign which read NO
TRESPASSING, then climbed the gravel bed up to the train
tracks. In one direction the tracks disappeared around
a bend. In the other they ran straight as far as I could
see. We were still only about fifty yards from my house,
and I thought if Mom began to measure the back windows she would see me and it would be better to throw
myself in front of the train than to have her send me to
my room so that Dad could "teach me a lesson" when he
came home from work.

Tack gave me half the toothpaste tubes. "Unscrew the
tops," he said, "and set each tube on the tracks with the
hole facing us."

"What for?" I asked.

"We're going to play like we are standing in front of a
firing squad," he said, "like captured spies. Just before
the train hits the tubes I'll holler, 'Ready, aim, fire!' And
when the toothpaste hits us we're dead."

"Cool," I said, and began to lay out my toothpaste tubes, positioning them so they'd blast us real
good. Tack finished laying his out, then leaned over
and placed his ear against the iron rail like a TV
Indian.

"I can hear one coming," he said.

I touched the rail and felt it vibrate, and then I
looked up and down the tracks until I could see a big
yellow engine round the bend.

"Get ready," Tack yelled. He pulled out a pack of

chocolate cigarettes and gave me one. I stuck it in the corner of my mouth. Then we took our positions side by side and stood as if tied to poles with our hands behind our backs. We were very brave with our chins thrust forward. We didn't wear blindfolds.

The train was about fifty yards away when Tack announced in a fake deep voice, "Do you traitors have any last words?" Just then, out of the corner of my eye, I saw Miss Kitty dragging herself up over the first rail.

"Stop!" I yelled, and lunged at the cat. Tack turned to see what I was doing and yanked me to the ground just as the train came roaring by. The engine hit the toothpaste tubes and we were both blasted. Tack rolled off me, clutching his heart. I jumped up and tried to find Miss Kitty. She wasn't on my side of the tracks and I had to wait until the train passed to see if she made it all the way across before the huge wheels got her.

I kept thinking, If she lives I promise to remove the bell. I'll let her eat any warm-blooded creature of her choice. I'll even let her chew on me. Please, please, please, I begged, let her live.

But once the train had passed, I couldn't find her. I searched along the tracks. I poked through the weeds. I kicked over a few big rocks. And then I found the copper cowbell, flattened out like a giant penny that had been set on the tracks. Attached to the bell was the collar, sliced clean through, with a little neck patch of bloody fur caught in the buckle.

"Oh my God," I shouted, and danced nervously around. "What happened to the cat?" I poked the piece of fur with the tip of my shoe. Maybe the wheel of the train had cut the collar clean off and the cat had run away. I told Tack what I was thinking.

"No chance," he replied as he took a fake puff off his chocolate cigarette. "That cat did not escape."

"Well, then, where did it go?"

"How do you think those train wheels stay greased?" he replied, then answered his own question. "Track kill."

I moaned, and while I was frantically looking around, Betsy had come out to see what we were up to.

"Why are you covered with toothpaste?" she asked.

"Firing squad," Tack said matter-of-factly, as if that would explain why we looked like toothpaste testers at the end of a long workday.

Just then Betsy spotted the flattened bell. "Did you put the cat on the tracks?" she asked, horrified.

"No," I said. "I love animals. I'd never do a thing like that."

"But you put the bell on the cat," she said. "I told you it was going to come to this."

"We don't know if it's dead," I cried out. "We only have the bell and collar and fur patch. It might have lived and run off."

"Believe it or not!" Betsy shouted, and looked up at the sky as if she were having a private conversation with

God. "Jack Henry killed the cat and is now trying to play innocent."

Well, if she was talking to God, I thought, He would know I was innocent. Maybe I was dumb, or maybe I had done something stupid, but I wasn't cruel.

I picked up the bell, the collar, and the little patch of bloody neck fur. "I'm sorry, Miss Kitty," I said, and petted the dirty fur with my fingertip. Then my eyes started welling up and I had to get out of there.

Later, in the back yard, I buried the piece of fur with the spot of blood on it. I put up a cross of twigs, and with a rusty nail scratched "Miss Kitty" on a stone which I pressed into the ground. "I'll never have another cat again," I whispered into the soft dirt. Then I turned and trudged across the back lawn. Pete followed. I had asked him to keep me company at the burial because I knew I was going to first feel sad, then guilty. After I took a few steps I said, "It should have been me who got hit by the train."

"That's what Betsy said," Pete replied.

"Don't you have a thought of your own?" I growled. After the guilt came anger.

"Why should I?" he said. "Betsy is smarter than all of us put together."

"I can't believe you listen to her propaganda," I said. "Betsy is no smarter than my little finger."

"She said you ate the cat," Pete declared.

I was stunned. "Ate it!" I screeched.

"She said the next war is going to be fought over food and that people have to be prepared to eat their pets."

"Where did she hear that?" I asked.

"Miss Fry," he replied. She was our crazy survivalist next-door neighbor who was gleefully preparing for the end of the world.

"Well, I didn't eat the cat," I said.

"Did it taste like chicken? Because if it does I'll have a bite."

"Are you listening to me?" I asked. "I didn't eat the cat."

"Betsy said you lie," he said. "So how do I know what you did?"

He was no help at making me feel better. Poor Miss Kitty, I thought. I kept wondering what had happened to the rest of her. It couldn't have been very pretty. And even though I wanted to believe that she had escaped and run off into the bushes to lead a long and happy life, I honestly didn't believe it. The only thing I knew for sure was that I didn't eat her.

I trudged through the back door and into the kitchen.

"Well look what the cat dragged in," Betsy sang tauntingly.

I groaned and covered my heart with my hand. "Can't you see I'm in emotional pain?" I said to her.

"What's emotional pain compared to being flattened

by a train? Besides," she added, "you should cheer up.
Just in case you are arrested for caticide, it says in the
newspaper that when criminals in prison are allowed to
keep cats in their cells they become nicer, less violent
people."

"Well, what happens to the cats?" I asked. "Do they
become meaner and more savage?"

"Believe it or not!" Betsy shouted up at the ceiling.
"Jack has asked a good question."

Just then there was a knock at the door.

"Make yourself useful," Betsy snarled, and jerked her
thumb toward the living room.

I opened the door. It was Tack Smith again. He was
all cleaned up and smiling nicely, and he had another
cat. Only this one wasn't scratching him up, it was just
sitting calmly at his feet. It was wearing a thin collar,
and Tack reached forward and offered me the leather
leash handle. Oh no, I thought, not this again, and I
stepped back.

"Brought you a replacement cat," he said cheerfully.
"Grandma picked it out herself."

"Did you tell her what happened to the first one?" I
asked, ready to slam the door on him and hide.

"Didn't have the guts," he replied. "Grandma just
had a pacemaker put in. It's one thing to lose a cat, but
another to lose your grandmother."

"Well, no dice on the cat," I said. "I've had it."

"Just hold your horses," he said. "I know you are going through cat mourning, but you have to calm down. This cat is smarter than a dog." He turned to the cat and commanded, "Roll over!"

The cat stretched out and rolled over.

"Bark!" he ordered.

To my surprise, the cat began to spit out a strange little bark.

Tack unhooked the leash. "Fetch," he hollered, throwing a stick across the yard. The cat ran after it and brought it back and dropped it at his feet, then obediently waited for him to throw it again.

"See," Tack said. "You'll love this cat. It's like a dog without being a dog."

I was beginning to think I could open my heart one more time and love this cat.

Just when I stooped down to pet it Betsy called out, "Does that cat know you killed the last one?"

"What it doesn't know won't hurt it," I replied.

"Why don't you take it out to the tracks and ask it to play dead?" she continued.

"I never meant to hurt that cat," I replied, defending myself.

"Hey," Betsy said, as she returned to her crossword puzzle. "What's a four-letter word for cat killer?"

I couldn't think of one.

"J-a-c-k," she spelled out.

"I'll get you," I said. "Cross my heart, I'll get you back."

"Sorry to burst your bubble, feline felon," Betsy said. "You couldn't get me back in ten lifetimes."

I had an awful feeling she was right. But it was okay. Because now I had the best cat in the world. I let out a sharp whistle. "Come on, Miss Kitty the Second," I commanded, and my dog-cat dutifully followed me up the hall to my room.

Science according to Mrs. Pierre.

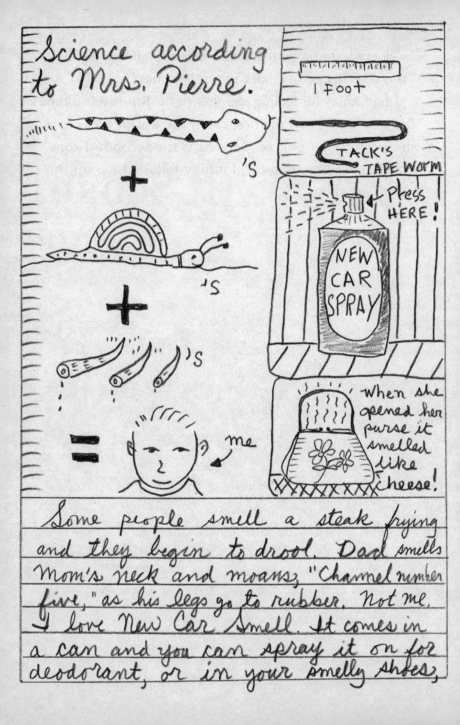

's

+

's

+

's

= me

1 FOOT

TACK'S TAPE WORM

Press HERE!

NEW CAR SPRAY

When she opened her purse it smelled like cheese!

Some people smell a steak frying and they begin to drool. Dad smells Mom's neck and moans, "Chanel number five," as his legs go to rubber. Not me, I love New Car Smell. It comes in a can and you can spray it on for deodorant, or in your smelly shoes,

The Sixth Sense

On the first day of class, our fifth-grade teacher, Mrs. Pierre, met each one of us at the door. *"Bonjour,"* she said enthusiastically, and shook each of our hands as we entered the classroom. "I look forward to a bea-u-ti-ful year with you. *Bonjour.* We are at the beginning of a new adventure. *Bonjour."* It didn't take me long to figure out she was head-over-heels in love with everything French.

It was already hot at eight in the morning and her shiny red lipstick had begun to spread into the tiny cracks above and below her lips. It gave them a furry look, and each time she sang *"Bonjour,"* they moved like two caterpillars.

"Bonjour," I said in return to her greeting. She smiled at me and this made me decide immediately that I liked her, and so I planned to sit as close to her desk as possible.

But she didn't allow us to choose our own seats, and instead made us gather in the front of the room. "Clap, clap," she said as she clapped her hands to get our attention. "I've arranged the seating chart according to gender. I find it best when boys and girls don't mix and distract one another. Boys are snakes and snails and puppy dogs' tails and need to fight among themselves. And girls are sugar and spice and everything nice and need their own *milieu*."

She had me confused. Did she really mean that all boys were disgusting and all girls were charming? Even my sister didn't believe that. The last time someone gave Betsy pink-colored clothes she cut them into strips and we used them for kite tails.

Down the middle of the room Mrs. Pierre had positioned tall bookshelves filled with books. I guessed that the boys' and girls' sides wouldn't be able to see each other except through the peeking spaces between the top of the books on one shelf and the bottom of the next shelf.

She began to assign all the girls to desks on the right side of the room and all the boys to the left. I ended up in a seat close to the back and next to the bookshelves. When she finished, she stood on an X-mark I had seen taped to the floor. The X was directly in line with the end of the bookshelves and just in front of the blackboard. In that one perfect spot all the boys could clearly see her, and so could all the girls. When she stood on the X and looked at the entire class her left eye was pulled way over toward the girls and her right eye was pulled way over toward the boys. It gave her the look of a hammerhead shark. Suddenly the red lipstick looked like the blood of her victims and I began to change my mind about liking her. I put her on "wait and see" status, which is what my mom does with people who she isn't sure of right away.

While I was thinking about the mysterious differences between boys and girls, Mrs. Pierre turned her back toward us and faced the blackboard. Above the alphabet letters on top of the board she had mounted a rearview mirror from a car so she could keep her eyes on us even as she wrote, and when she did write it was amazing. She put a piece of chalk in each hand and stretched them out as far as she could. Then she started writing with both hands at the same time. Her left hand wrote normally from the beginning of the sentence to the right. Her right hand was incredible. She started with the period of the sentence, and then with the last letter of the last word, and continued to write completely backward from right to left. She did this with ease, and she did it all in *cursive,* and she finished the sentence exactly in the middle where her two hands met and seamlessly completed the final word.

I felt my lips move in awe as I read, "The education of the senses is the foundation of civilization."

Writing a sentence from both ends and finishing it in

the middle was an amazing skill. I may have hated the way the room was organized, and I hated being thought of as nasty just because I was a boy, but her handwriting made me like her again.

"Does anyone know what this means?" she asked as each of her protruding, independent eyes scanned us.

She pointed to someone on the girls' side. "Stand up, please."

"It means, Mrs. Pierre," the girl said with a fake French accent, "that without an understanding of our senses there would be no civilization."

"*Oui! Oui! Oui!*" Mrs. Pierre cried out, as if she were the little piggy toe that cried all the way home. She paused and composed herself by smoothing the wrinkles out of her skirt with the palms of her hands. "Without knowing *who* you are, you will never know *why* you do what you do. So for the next five days of school we will work on educating the five senses. Smell, hearing, touch, taste, and sight. The beauty of educating all five senses is that you get the sixth for free. Now who can tell me what the sixth sense is?" she asked. Once again her ball-bearing eyes worked independently of each other as she scanned the class.

"A spooky feeling like when a ghost enters a room?" some guy said.

"Déjà vu?" said a girl I couldn't see.

"You can sense danger?" another guy guessed.

Mrs. Pierre smiled. "No, no, no," she said. "You are trying too hard. Here is one of nature's greatest gifts. Once you educate the five senses you develop the most important sense of all, the sense of *good taste*."

I could hear a few confused kids smacking their lips.

"I don't mean *good taste* as with your tongue. I mean *good taste* as in good manners, how to dress, how to think, how to live, how to be sophisticated and *civilized*."

I loved getting things for free, and it sounded like a great secret that after you got the five senses under control the sense of *good taste* came as a bonus. Sure, I thought, she's different, but no other teacher I ever had cared enough to really want to educate us about ourselves.

"And then, students," she said, and clapped her hands together as if they were a pair of cymbals, "we will apply our sharpened senses to create only what comes from refined civilizations—great literature. For, as the French say, 'Literature is the fruit of the senses.' "

I perked up when she said she wanted us to write. I was hoping to get a teacher who allowed us to keep journals. But then I slumped back down into my seat when she announced, "So, tonight your homework is to work on the sense of smell. Tomorrow, arrive wearing a perfume or cologne that smells *heavenly*." When she said *heavenly* her nose flared, her eyelids fluttered, and her knees buckled. I thought she was going to faint. But she pulled out of it and before long we were learning how to name our senses in French.

After school I opened my journal and leafed through. It was the kind that had a wise saying printed on the top of each page, and I was looking for something to inspire me. *A lesson is something someone teaches you,* one read. *An insight is something you teach yourself.* I couldn't think of an *insight* I had discovered on my own. It seemed to me that everything I knew was taught to me by someone else. I figured it was about time I grew up and figured some stuff out on my own. Suddenly, I remembered my sense-of-smell assignment, so I put my journal down and got moving.

The next morning I was coming out of the bathroom when Betsy passed me in the hall.

"What is that smell?" she hooted.

"What smell?" I replied innocently.

She leaned forward and sniffed my neck and ears and shirt, then she paused. "I've got it," she exclaimed. "It's new-car smell!"

"It's just some cologne I'm wearing for show-and-tell," I said blandly.

"Where did you get it?"

"The car-parts store," I said. "New-car smell is one of my favorite smells and I can get it in a spray can."

"You're nuts," she said. "I love anchovies but I don't rub them all over myself."

"Well, you should," I snapped back. "It might help improve your social life."

"Your teacher is going to adore you," Betsy mumbled acidly as she marched into the bathroom and slammed the door.

At school Mrs. Pierre had us line up at the door. She sniffed the first girl in line. "White Shoulders," she announced, naming the perfume. "Am I correct?"

"Yes," the girl replied, amazed as if her deepest secret had been revealed.

Then Mrs. Pierre sniffed us one after another, showing off her "olfactory intelligence," as she called it.

"Old Spice. Shalimar. Canoe. Joy. English Leather," she rattled off. "Chanel No. 5, good choice," she said, patting a girl on her head. "Shows excellent French taste." Then she smelled me. Her nose got closer and closer until the tip of it was pressed down inside my shirt collar. Finally she pulled back and said, "I give up. What is that?"

"New-car smell," I said proudly, and reached into my book bag and removed the spray can.

"Well," she said, bewildered. "That certainly is *tasteful*." She looked over at the girls and rolled her eyes. *"Boys,"* she groaned. "Their creativity is without limits."

I smiled weakly. At least she thought wearing new-car smell was creative.

Mrs. Pierre leaned forward and smelled the next kid. But then she said her nose was clogged up and she quit without naming the perfume.

As I shuffled toward my desk, a couple guys gave me the thumbs-up, which made me feel better. But I knew the teacher thought I was still an uncivilized boy made of snakes and snails.

After everyone had settled down, Mrs. Pierre stood on the X at the front of the class and tapped the side of her nose with one finger. "See," she said. "The sense of smell can be trained. By the end of the year you will be able to tell, even in the dark, just who is who in this room . . . especially if they smell like a car."

Then she blew her nose with so much force it made the sound of heavy furniture being dragged across a rough floor. Carefully she unfolded the tissue and examined what she had expelled. She had a look on her face of a psychic examining tea leaves. It was as though she was reading a message about her future. It must have been good because she smiled broadly before closing the tissue and slipping it into her pocket.

That night I pulled out my journal and had a sudden insight. I knew I was growing older because I could weigh both Mrs. Pierre's good and bad qualities and come up with a sense of what I liked or disliked about her. When I was younger I could only pick out one thing about a person and get stuck on that. If a person was funny, I'd like them no matter if they were serial killers, and if a person had the annoying habit of chewing gum like a cow then I didn't care for them even though they might be a saint. So even though Mrs. Pierre didn't love my cologne, I still liked her idea about educating the senses.

We were next assigned to bring something to represent our sense of sound. I wanted to please Mrs. Pierre. I didn't want her to think I was a complete moron, so I gave the assignment some careful thought. We had a record with French children's songs and so I listened to it over and over and practiced singing.

The next day Mrs. Pierre called on me first. I knew she would because I had been so weird with my sense of smell. But I was ready for her.

I stood up and sang, *"Frère Jacques, Frère Jacques, Dormez-vous, dormez-vous . . ."* And I finished the whole song in French.

Mrs. Pierre was even more wide-eyed than usual. "Bravo! Bravo!" she shouted, and began to clap. "Please," she beckoned me, "step to the front of the class and take a bow."

I did. I bent over and peeked out at the girls' side. They were smiling and clapping. Then I looked over at the boys' side. They were clapping as if a gun was held to their heads. Suddenly, I had another insight. Mrs. Pierre was right. Girls are nice and supportive and boys always try to make everyone feel like a jerk. I had always figured that kids who did everything the teacher asked were just brownnosers trying to get a better grade. Now, it seemed that they were not brownnosers, they were smart kids who were trying really hard to learn what the teacher was getting at.

When I came home from school I found Betsy in the kitchen, working on the crossword puzzle.

"Did you ever have an insight?" I asked Betsy.

She looked up at me and frowned. "Give me an example," she said.

"Like I used to think brownnosers were jerks but now I understand where they are coming from and I want to be one of them."

"Interesting," she mused. "I think I'm having an *insight* right now."

"Really?" I said. "That is so cool. What are you thinking?"

"That you have bugged me in the past. That you are bugging me now. And you will continue—in your unrelenting way—to bug me for the rest of my life," she said.

"That's too obvious to be an insight," I said, catching on that she was making fun of me. "You have to try harder."

"How's this," she said, and held her temples and squinted. "In about thirty seconds you'll either be out of my sight or dead."

"Okay, okay," I moaned. "I just thought you'd like to know that I'm getting smarter."

"I hate to be the one to inform you," she said. "But

you must be the last person on the planet to figure out that if you do what the teacher assigns, and put some effort into the job, you will learn something."

"Better late than never," I sang out.

"What's a five-letter word for beat it?" she asked.

"S-c-r-a-m," I spelled out as I dashed down the hall.

The rest of the week I did exactly what Mrs. Pierre expected. For the sense of taste I brought in french fries but I called them *pommes frites*. She loved that. And for the sense of sight I brought in a library book on the French painter Monet. She thought I was wonderful and went on and on about what a genius Monet was and how I had a very refined eye for "art appreciation." And for the sense of touch I brought in Betsy's fake ponytail because it was in the shape of a French twist. Mrs. Pierre loved it. She even tried it on for the class.

At the end of the fifth day, after everyone had finished their show-and-tell for the sense of touch, Mrs. Pierre took her place on the X and gave us the last assignment.

"Now that we have mastered the senses, I want you to write a story about something memorable. And, I want you to use all of your senses when writing the story, so when I read it I can smell, feel, taste, hear, and touch what you are talking about."

Okay, I thought to myself. This is the time for me to really show her what I can do.

It was a Friday night but I was ready to get to work. I had given some thought to the story I had wanted to write and was eager to get started. It was about something incredible that had happened to me the week before and it involved all my senses. I went into my room, pulled out my diary, and got busy.

THE UGLY THING
by Jack Henry

My friend Tack Smith called me up on the telephone. "Come over to my house," he said all out of breath (SOUND). "I just got back from the doctor's and have something awesome for you to see (SIGHT)."

"Okay," I said, even though I really didn't want to. Something weird had recently happened at his house. His mom and dad had split up. But instead of going their separate ways they only walked across the street. Tack's dad had traded wives with the man, Mr. Butters, who lived directly across the road. Or you could say that Tack's mom and Mrs. Butters had traded husbands. Either way, it was very weird at his house, and even though Tack hadn't talked about it I knew it had to be strange for him. The only thing he had said was that he woke up in his own bed and showered and dressed then carried his dirty clothes across the street where his real mom fed him breakfast.

So, when he asked me to come over I thought it was my duty as a friend. Everyone thought that he had been getting sick and skinny because he was depressed from the parent-swap deal, but it turns out that he had a tapeworm in his belly. I figured he had saved it and wanted me to see it.

I had put on my yellow plastic raincoat in case the visit got messy, but Mom stopped me and made me put on something decent. She said that the new mom was trash and she didn't want me looking like trash too. Mom called her a "gold digger" because since she moved in with Tack's dad she made him buy her a new Cadillac, install central air-conditioning, and lay multi-colored shag wall-to-wall carpet in the house. So I left my door on my way to Tack's to see his tapeworm as if I were dressed for church. I walked the twenty-five feet to his front door and took a deep breath and knocked. Just in case the new mom was spying on me through the peephole I hummed a church hymn and twiddled my thumbs in a circle like a well-mannered choirboy. But Tack was waiting for me. He whipped the door open. "You look like a Bible salesman," he said. "Come down to my bedroom and feast your eyes on the Eighth Wonder of the World."

As we darted through the living room his new mom looked up from her HOUSE BEAUTIFUL magazine and gave me a tight-lipped glare as though she had been waiting forever in a doctor's office. It seemed she was in a lot of pain so I just waved and kept walking. Tack's room was the same as it ever was—a total blowout wreck that was so dirty my mom would have had a heart attack. I loved it. Books were piled up as high as the curtain rods. Every animal cage he ever had was still there, including a few of the animals that were dried out like tiny mummies. A mobile of wired-together animal bones clattered in a circle overhead as they spun from the blade of a ceiling fan.

There was a mayonnaise jar sitting on his bed. Inside was something that looked like a giant rubber band. I couldn't make out a head or tail. "Awesome," I remarked, pointing at it.

"Seven feet long," he said, raising his shirt and rubbing his sunken belly.

"How'd you get it?" I asked, wanting to avoid the same fate.

"Raw hamburger meat," he explained. "I used to eat bits and pieces of it out of the bowl as my real mom mixed it up."

I thought Tack's real mom might have sent his new mom some raw hamburger and now she had a tapeworm which is why she looked so grumpy.

Tack began to unscrew the jar. "Let's measure it," he said. "I want to be sure. Maybe it is a world record and I can be famous." He fished the end of the worm out with two fingers and began to gently unravel a piece of it across the bedsheet. It smelled like pickle juice (SMELL).

I spotted a ruler on his desk. I got it and began to hold it against the white worm. "How'd you know it was in you?" I asked.

"Stool sample," he replied. "The doctor gave me something that looked like a Tupperware container and I had to poop in it and take it to a lab. They did some tests and the doctor called and told my mom."

"How'd they get it out?" I asked, imagining they might have had to use a long pair of tweezers.

"Poison," he said and made a yucky face. "The taste almost killed me."

"Then what?" I asked.

"It died in my belly," he said, "and I pooped it out."

"Gross," I shrieked, and felt my butt pucker up (TOUCH). "What did it feel like coming out?"

"The only thing I could think of at the time," he said, "is once I was picking my nose and I got the hard, crusty part of a booger between my fingers and slowly began to pull it out. And as I did so I could feel something tickling me way up behind the corner of my eye. And as I pulled I felt the tail of the booger slide all the way down the inside of my nose till I had it out. It was all jelly white like a squid tentacle and about four inches long. My biggest booger ever. And that is what the worm felt like, a cold tickle."

I could hardly believe what he had just said. I stood there looking at his face, and then at the worm, and back at his face again.

"Wow," I said. I just didn't know what else to say. It was all so weird. Then finally I said, "What are you going to do with it?"

"Eat it," he replied ghoulishly. "Give it a taste of its own medicine."

He took a knife and fork out of his desk drawer and sliced off an inch.

"Are you joking?" I asked, wide-eyed.

"No," he said. "I asked you over so you'd be a witness when I told everyone at school."

"Okay," I said. "I'm watching."

He reached into his desk and pulled out a little paper packet of salt. He poured some on, then quickly sucked the piece of *worm off the fork and swallowed (*TASTE*). "Gave him a taste of his own medicine," he remarked.*

"That is sick," I said. "Sick, sick, sick."

"Excellent," he said, and grinned. "Just remember, I'm the number-one sicko in this neighborhood." He held up his pointer finger like a champion. "Number one and don't you forget it."

Suddenly I had an insight. I figured Tack was fooling me. "That wasn't a worm," I said. "That was really spaghetti!"

He smiled. "Good guess, Henry. We have a new pasta machine that can make a spaghetti strand from here to the moon." He opened another drawer and pulled out a baby-food jar. "This is the real worm," he said, frowning. "Only about a foot long. But saying it was seven feet and all made for a better story."

"Well, a tapeworm is pretty gross no matter how big."

"I wanted the world record," he said. "I was going for twenty feet."

"Eat some more raw meat and give it a shot," I said.

"Not yet," he said. "First I'll have to fatten up, or there will be nothing left of me but a big, drippy worm."

THE END

The next day I walked up to Mrs. Pierre's desk first thing and turned in the story. "I really worked hard on this one," I said. "I hope you like it."

"I'm sure I will," she chirped. "You have such good taste."

"You smell very nice today," I said. "Is your perfume French?"

"It is. Very perceptive of you," she replied.

"You have a little lipstick on your teeth," I whispered, trying to be discreet.

She slipped her tongue across her teeth and wiped them clean. I was so eager to be polite I said, "You're welcome," before she even had time to say thank you.

When I turned around there was some guy staring at me. I knew the look. It meant, I can't stand your guts, you low-life teacher's pet. I used to stare at brownnosing kids exactly the same way. But that was before I changed my tune and started working with my teacher instead of against her.

All day I kept imagining Mrs. Pierre reading my story and laughing, then standing in front of the class and reading it out loud as an example of "the fruit of the senses." I even imagined that she would allow me to sit on the girls' side because I had proven that I was a boy *not* made of snakes and snails and puppy dogs' tails.

When it was time for afternoon recess Mrs. Pierre kept me behind. I smiled up at her and got ready to be praised.

"I read your story," she said coldly. "And I was appalled. Shocked. Mortified! It is in the *worst* taste possible."

I was shocked too. "What's wrong with it?" I asked.

"It is everything—the beginning, middle, and end.

Simply, it is bad manners to write such a story. You should be ashamed."

She thrust it back toward me as if it were a pair of smelly socks.

"I'm going to be working late tonight," she said. "I would very much like to discuss your inappropriate work with your parents."

"I'm not sure I can get them to come," I said, worried.

"Well, see what you can do," she pressed. "Otherwise I will have no choice but to grade your story harshly."

"Okay," I said. And because I was still trying to please her I added "goodbye" in French.

She didn't answer.

We were sitting at the dining-room table. My plate was piled high with fish sticks floating in a puddle of creamed corn. I was nervous because I knew I was going to have to ask Mom or Dad to meet with Mrs. Pierre.

"You haven't touched your food," Mom observed. "Looks like you lost your best friend." She must have seen the stunned expression on my face.

"My teacher hated my story," I said quietly.

"Why, honey?" Mom asked.

"She said it was in bad taste," I replied.

"Bad taste?" Betsy asked, incredulous. "You get graded for bad taste? I'd love to have your teacher. I bet she failed you for something because you have the worst taste of anyone I know."

"Well, what did you write about?" Mom asked.

"Tack's tapeworm," I said, and shrugged. "No big deal."

"Gross!" said Pete.

"Hey, tapeworms are not in bad taste," Dad said. "I could tell you some stories that are in really bad taste."

"Let's not," Mom said, giving him the evil eye.

"The point is," Dad said, "there are good stories and lousy stories. Taste has nothing to do with it."

"Writing about gross things shows bad judgment," Mom continued with me, ignoring Dad. "There is no reason you have to discuss this issue in class when there are so many uplifting stories to tell. Why not write about how your sister won that beauty contest in North Carolina."

"That would just be *bad* writing," I groaned. Pete laughed.

"No kidding," said Betsy. "You couldn't possibly capture my beauty with the way you butcher the English language."

"She wants a parent meeting tonight to discuss it," I said, finally getting to the point.

"I just got home from work," Mom said. "Can't Mrs. Pierre do it some other time?"

"I'll take you," Dad said. "I have to swing by the Elks Club anyway, so we can drop by the school first."

"Thanks," I said.

On the way over in the car Dad quietly worked a toothpick around between his teeth.

"Hey, Dad, did you ever have an insight about life?" I asked.

"Yeah," he replied. "I had one. And that was all I needed. When I was about your age I figured out that I could either do and say the things I thought of. Or I'd end up doing and saying the things other people thought of for me. It was that simple."

I knew just what he was talking about. And suddenly I had an insight. Dad said what he said because he knew just what I was going through and he was coming to the rescue. I reached over and gave him a tap on the shoulder.

Dad smiled. "You're a chip off the old block," he said. "Now don't worry about tonight. You just let me do the talking and watch how a *pro* handles this situation."

When we came marching through the classroom door Mrs. Pierre had just finished putting on a fresh coat of lipstick and was slipping the tube back into her purse.

"Nice to meet you," Dad said, and pointed directly at her mouth. "You got some lipstick on your teeth." Then, before she could say a word, he got right down to business. "Now what is the problem with Jack's story?"

Mrs. Pierre hesitated. I could tell she felt awkward talking about me in front of my face.

"I'll be right back," I said. I stepped out of the door-way and stopped around the corner. I could hear every-thing they said.

"Jack is a good storyteller," Mrs. Pierre said. "But his subject matter is simply in poor taste. He was doing so well. I didn't expect this sort of thing from him. I expected something more *tasteful*. He's a good boy, with good manners . . ."

"Well, you know what they say," Dad said. "Good taste starts in the home."

"I agree," she said.

"So let me tell you a little story and this way you'll get a sense of where Jack is coming from."

"Fine," she said.

Dad pulled out a pack of cigarettes. "Want one?" he asked. She refused. Dad lit up, took a puff, and when I peeked around the doorjamb I watched as he blew two cones of smoke out of his nose like a fuming bull. I had seen him do this at the Elks Club when all the men had gathered around to hear him tell a story.

"So," he started, as he slid the metal trash can over for an ashtray. "Once upon a time there was a very fat man who kept eating and eating but he kept getting skinnier and skinnier. Finally he goes to the doctor. 'Doctor, Doctor,' he says, 'what's wrong with me?' So the doctor listens to the symptoms and examines the man and says, 'You have a tapeworm.' The man is surprised and says to the doctor, 'Well, how do I get rid of it?' The doctor says, 'Go home and every day for six days in a row shove an apple and a hard-boiled egg up your rear end. Then on the seventh day just shove the apple up.' "

Dad took a drag off his cigarette as he looked over at Mrs. Pierre. She seemed stunned and I could just imagine she was thinking, "Like father, like son." Or, "The apple doesn't fall far from the tree."

"What about the hard-boiled egg?" I blurted out, and stepped back into the room.

"That's just what the man said to the doctor," Dad replied, and gave me a wink and a smile. "And the doctor says, 'That's just what the tapeworm is thinking. And the moment it sticks its head out and says, "Hey, where's my egg?" Splat! You hit it with a hammer.' "

After the punch line Dad threw his head back and had a long, hard laugh. I wanted to, but didn't because I also wanted to get a clear look at Mrs. Pierre's face. It wasn't that she was appalled or angry. She seemed confused, that people could listen to something so tasteless and find it so much fun.

Finally, Mrs. Pierre pulled herself together. "Well," she said, and stood up. "Thank you for the story, and for coming in this evening. I have a much better sense of where Jack gets his ideas."

Dad smiled. "It was a pleasure meeting you," he said. "And if Jack ever misbehaves, you give me a call. I don't care what he writes. But he'd better mind his manners."

I waved to Mrs. Pierre and she waved in return.

On the way home Dad looked over at me. "You do everything she tells you to do," he said. "She's your teacher, so she's the boss. But when you have a good story, then you be the boss. Never let other people put words in your mouth. You got that?"

"Loud and clear," I said.

"And no more brownnosing," he said. "It's embarrassing to the family."

I smiled at him and rubbed the palm of my hand across my nose. "Hey, Dad," I said. "Where'd you get that story?"

"I got a million of 'em," he said, full of high spirits. "Let's go down to the Elks Club. Keep your ears open and you'll have another story in no time."

I looked over at his face and could see he was already thinking of a story to tell the other men. He was great, and I wanted to be just like him.

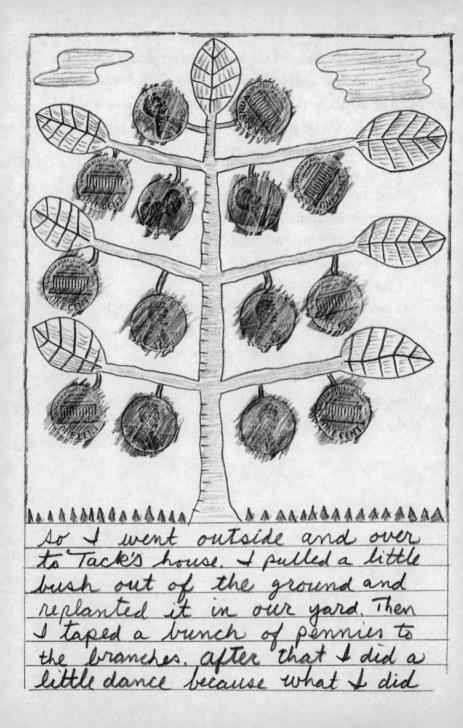

so I went outside and over
to Tack's house. I pulled a little
bush out of the ground and
replanted it in our yard. Then
I taped a bunch of pennies to
the branches. After that I did a
little dance because what I did

The Penny Tree

"What are you getting Pete for his birthday?" Betsy asked. He was going to be five years old and I hadn't gotten him a thing.

"I'm still thinking about it," I answered, as I wedged my hand between the couch cushions.

"You are not *thinking*," Betsy shot back. "You are couch fishing for change because you're broke."

"I've got plenty of cash," I replied, lying as my fingers desperately clawed the mysterious spaces within the couch.

"You spend all your money on yourself and that nutty cat," she said, reading my mind. I had just spent my last cent on a blue rhinestone Chihuahua collar for Miss Kitty II, who, as Tack said, was the doggiest cat in the world.

"Ah ha!" I shouted, and pulled an old penny out of the crack. "Now I've got something for Pete." I held the penny up for her to see. "This little penny will change his life," I announced, without the slightest idea how it might do so. But I kept talking. "You don't need a lot of cash to give a great gift." I rapped my knuckles against my head. "You just need a generous imagination."

"That's just another way of saying you are cheap!" she said, sneering.

"Just you wait," I snapped back. "With this one penny I will steal the birthday gift-giving show."

"Put your money where your mouth is," she said. "I bet ten bucks—that's a thousand pennies—that my gift will be his favorite."

"You're on," I replied, thinking that I did need a "generous imagination." Quick.

I grabbed the classified section of the newspaper off the coffee table and went into my bedroom. What can I buy for a penny, I wondered, as I stared at the ads. Cars were too expensive. I turned the page. Houses, furniture, and exotic pets were out of my price range. There was nothing for a penny at the grocery store, shoe store, toy store, bookstore—any store. In fact, nothing in Miami could be bought for a penny. Why do they even make them? I asked myself. They just end up behind couch cushions, in jars, jammed into penny loafers, lost under refrigerators, sucked into vacuum cleaners, or swallowed by crawling babies. They certainly were a lot more trouble than they were worth.

Buying something for a penny was definitely out of the question. I was back to where I started. But then I glanced at one more ad. A plant store was having a sale. Still, even a bag of dirt, which I could get for free in my back yard, cost two dollars. Even a jug of tap water was more than my budget could handle. Then suddenly my generous imagination saved the day.

After dinner Mom brought out the birthday cake. She lit the five candles and said to Pete, "Honey, make a wish."

Pete's eyes floated up toward the ceiling as he sucked a whole roomful of air into his lungs, then he leaned forward. The five little flames didn't know what hit them. In a split second there was nothing left but five vanishing trails of smoke.

"Okay," Pete announced, grinning. "I'm ready to open presents."

Mom and Dad lifted a big box onto the table. Small trains crisscrossed the wrapping paper. Pete ripped it open with one swipe and lifted the top off the box. There was a train set with a steam locomotive and lots of old-time cattle cars, and water tankers and a red caboose.

"Awesome!" Pete shrieked, and threw his arms around Mom and Dad. "Thank you," he said.

Mom and Dad spent a lot more than a penny, but I

wasn't worried. My generous imagination had been extra generous.

Suddenly Pete turned toward Betsy. "Next," he said.

She gave him a big package with a huge bow on the top. Pete yanked the bow off, peeled the paper back, and flipped open the top of a box. He pulled out a pair of train engineer's striped bib overalls, a matching denim cap, and a red bandanna.

"You are the best sister on the planet," he said, and gave her a hug. I figured she must have spent at least twenty bucks.

Then he looked at me. I felt my ears turn red. The heat was on. I supposed if I hadn't spent all my money on things like a self-cleaning cat box I would be giving him a pocket watch or a silver-plated railroad spike or something that would fit the gift-giving theme. Still, I didn't lose faith in my generous imagination.

"So," Betsy cut in with her smarmy voice, "what did you get Pete?"

I reached into my shirt pocket and removed a small manila envelope. On the front of it I had drawn a tree covered with tiny pennies. Under the drawing I had written: One Penny-Tree Seed.

I handed it to him. He opened the metal clasp and shook out the single penny and a piece of paper with "Planting Instructions." He looked suspiciously at the penny, then back at me. Then Mom and Dad and Betsy stared at me. They did not seem pleased with my choice of gifts.

I snatched the Planting Instructions out of his hand. "It reads, 'Plant in fertile soil and water six times daily until a penny tree grows.' "

"Will it actually grow?" he asked.

"Oh yeah," I shot back. "Absolutely. It's guaranteed. Says so right on the directions."

"Wow!" he shouted. "This is the best gift ever. When the tree grows I'll have enough pennies to buy an entire real train."

"Sure you will," I said, with my generous imagination getting away from me. "You could even buy the old Santa Fe Railroad and ride it across the desert."

Then he ran out the back door to go plant his seed.

"Jack," Mom said, "I hope you haven't started something you will regret. Your brother believes everything you say, so don't you dare let him down."

"Don't worry," I said to Mom. "It's under control."

As soon as she was out of the room I turned to Betsy and stuck out my hand. "That will be one thousand pennies, please."

She gave me a jar of change and a few bills. "Mark my words. When you mess this up, this money is coming right back, plus another ten."

"We'll see," I replied.

The next morning Pete woke before me. When I got up I peeked out the kitchen window. There he was, watering his seed. I smiled to myself as I poured milk on my cereal. What an incredible gift, I thought. This was definitely the smartest thing I had ever cooked up. It only cost me one free cent, and on top of it I made a thousand more from Betsy. I felt like a genius. As I ate, I began to imagine what dog items I'd buy next for the cat.

When Pete came in he was excited. "I think it is growing already," he said.

"Could be," I replied. "Just remember, water it six times a day or else it will shrivel up and die." I figured he'd never be able to keep up the six times per day schedule and sooner or later I'd have to announce the death of the penny tree. And I will be blameless. It was perfect.

But the first warning I had that Pete's generous imagination was bigger than mine was when he came running up to me holding the windup alarm clock in his outstretched hands.

"How many hours apart is it if I water six times per day?" he asked.

I did the math in my head. "Four," I replied.

"Then set this for four hours from now," he said.

I did. When I handed it back to him he grabbed his little plastic play chair and went outside. When I looked out the window again he was sitting in his chair, reading a book with the alarm clock on his lap and the watering can at his side. Cute, I thought. Very cute. I should take a picture.

"Where's Pete?" Mom asked. "We have to go to the store and get more train track."

"Out back," I said, and pointed toward the window.

She looked out. "Oh, that is precious," she said. But then her voice grew serious. "Jack, you know your brother still believes in Santa Claus, the Easter Bunny, and the tooth fairy. It would be awful of you to burst his bubble."

"He's a little brother," I said. "It's a law that older brothers have to burst the bubbles of little brothers."

"Just don't hurt him," she warned me. "Or there is a parent's law that says there might be consequences."

That was her favorite warning, "There might be consequences." This always got my generous imagination worked up. Usually I pictured myself wrapped in chains and handcuffed to a post in our spider-filled attic.

That night the alarm went off at midnight, and again at four in the morning. Each time, Pete hopped out of bed, turned on his flashlight, and ran outside to water his penny tree. Each time, I had to set the alarm for him.

By morning, I was beginning to feel the "consequences" creeping up on me.

All the next day Pete kept up his watering routine, and I kept my mouth shut. That night we were sitting in the living room reading. Pete had pulled out his old copy of *The Carrot Seed*. He knew the story by heart and flipped through the pages over and over. "This is the greatest book ever," he shouted. "The little boy plants a carrot seed and waters it and waters it and even though everyone in his family says it won't grow he still waters it because *he* believes it will. And then, *boom,* overnight it grows into a giant carrot. That's just how it is going to be with my penny tree because *I* believe in it!"

I peeked over the top of my book. Mom, Dad, and Betsy were peeking up over their books—and they were glaring at me. I smiled back. They didn't.

Suddenly, I was beginning to feel bad about myself. Maybe I had gone too far. Maybe Pete was too delicate for my scheme. "I'll be right back," I announced, and put my book down. I ran to the garage and got a garden spade. Then I went over to Tack Smith's yard and dug up a plant that sort of looked like a little tree. Then I replanted it where Pete had planted his seed. I sneaked back into my bedroom and got a handful of pennies and some tape, then went back outside. Quickly, I taped a few pennies on the branches. "This will make him happy," I said to myself, "and then we can forget about the penny tree."

The next morning Pete woke me by jumping up and down on my bed and shouting. "It grew! It grew! I'm rich. Come see."

I hopped up and followed him outside. "Wow," I said, and made my eyes get real big. "It worked."

He bent down and held one in his hands. "Why are they held on with tape?" he asked.

"That's not tape," I said. "Those are penny stems."

"Cool," he said. Then he asked a question that I gave

the wrong answer to. "If I leave them on the tree will they grow really big, like huge penny hubcaps?"

"Nah," I replied. "They'll turn into nickels."

Pete's eyes bugged out. "Nickels!" he shouted. "Then I'll wait to pick them."

Oh no, I thought. I did it again.

Everything went downhill fast from there. And the more broke I became, the happier everyone else was. First, I had to sneak out in the middle of the night and change the pennies to nickels. And of course Pete was thrilled. When he saw them he danced a little dance around the yard and then announced that he would wait for them to become dimes. Once again, I dug into my piggy bank and got dimes and later sneaked out and put them on the tree. The following morning Pete went nuts. He did somersaults across the yard and drooled all over himself. Then he decided to hold out for quarters. That night, I changed the dimes to quarters. The next day Pete went screaming wildly around the back yard until he was so dizzy he fell over and announced he would wait for fifty-cent pieces. I had seen it coming, so I'd gotten Mom to exchange the money I'd won from Betsy for half dollars at the bank. That night I did the changeover. The next day he was bonkers. I tried to get him to pluck the half dollars off the tree, but no, he was holding out for the dollar bills. That night, I gave the half dollars back to Mom for singles. I taped ten bills all over the tree, and when I finished I said to myself, "Okay, I've broken even—this madness has got to stop. I started it, so I'll finish it."

I got a small pair of scissors and cut off all the leaves from the tree and left them scattered under the tiny branches.

The next morning Pete and I got up together to water the tree. On the way out of the house he said, "Maybe after the single-dollar bills there will be five-dollar bills, then tens, then twenties, then hundreds . . ." I stopped him. "Don't count your chickens before they are hatched," I warned him, sounding like my father.

When we arrived at the tree Pete gasped and dropped to his knees. "It died!" he shouted. "All its leaves fell off." He began to cry.

"But dollar bills are still left on the bare branches," I pointed out.

"Why'd it die?" he blubbered. "I loved this tree."

"It's not dead," I said, putting my arm around his shoulders. "It's just that winter is coming. The penny tree has a short growing season. You know, like oranges and limes."

Pete wiped his eyes on his sleeve. Then he thought about what I'd said. He thought about it for so long that I knew I was in trouble.

"You mean it will return next summer?" he asked.

"Yes," I said. "Of course it will."

"That is so cool!" he shouted. "I'll be rich all over again."

He was ripping the dollar bills off the tree as I stood up and slowly walked back to my room. I shook my piggy bank. It was empty. I better start saving now, I thought. That kid's generous imagination is going to cost me every red cent I can get my hands on.

There was a loud "crack"
sound and a bolt of lighten-
-ing hit the T.V. We dove across
the room as the T.V. began to
smoke. Mom came running in
and told us to put on rubber shoes.

From the Grave

Halloween didn't wait until dark to be spooky. It was a rainy Saturday morning and Pete and I were watching a *Hogan's Heroes* rerun on TV. Sergeant Carter had just set off explosives in an important Nazi railroad tunnel and was now dodging German patrols when suddenly a local TV announcer came on and said, "We interrupt this program to bring you an important news flash from the Dade County Sheriff's Department." But before he could deliver the news, there was a big bang and the house jumped as if hit by a truck. Mom screamed in the laundry room, and on television the announcer's face began to cloud over with wisps of white smoke that seemed to be leaking out of his shirt collar as if he were the devil's newscaster. Then the picture vanished, but the smoke stayed and gathered into a cloud as dark and thick as the ones above our house. I leapt forward and yanked the plug out of the wall just as Mom dashed into the room.

"We've been hit by lightning," she said breathlessly.

"The TV blew up!" Pete shouted, pointing at the smoke that was seeping, like an escaping ghost, out of the speaker at the front of the set. "We were going to get special news and it blew."

"Well, they were probably going to warn us of a lightning storm," Mom said. "I hope nothing else got zapped." She left the room to check.

I didn't think the Sheriff's Department would warn us about lightning storms. It had to be something else. Something menacing, like a runaway train full of deadly nerve gas, or a foreign invasion, but now we wouldn't know. I hopped up and looked out the window to see if UFO's were landing, or if a tidal wave was about to squish us like a giant hand. But I didn't spot anything abnormal, so I patrolled from window to window to see if the outside of the house was on fire from the lightning strike. I hoped it wasn't. I had big, all-day Halloween plans. Tack and I were going waterskiing. His older brother, Jock, who Tack called Jock Itch, had bought a used car and said he would take us with him. I had never water-skied before and wanted to try it, but since it was storming out I knew Mom wouldn't let me go. I peered through the back window, up at the sky. The clouds were still heavy and gray as stones, but they were breaking up. The sun was peeking through the cracks and the rain had stopped. Just then there was a knock at the door.

"That's for me," I yelled. I sprinted down the hall, across the living room, and whipped the door open. It was orange-haired Miss Fry and she thrust Miss Kitty II right up into my face. I knew this was going to be another car problem. Miss Kitty II loved cars. She had jumped into car windows, dropped into truck beds and convertibles from trees, and even chased them down the street like a dog.

"Is this your cat?" Miss Fry barked. She knew it was.

I casually reached for the tag around Miss Kitty II's neck, and examined it. "Yeah," I said.

"Well, I wish you would keep her from sleeping in my car. I got in just now and she crept up on my neck and batted my earrings and nearly scared me half to death. I thought a car-jacker was in the back seat. I almost had a coronary."

"I'm sorry," I said, staring at her miniature handcuff earrings. "But she really likes cars."

"Then maybe you should *buy* her one," Miss Fry suggested. She must have thought she said something very clever because her hips started to gyrate as if she were spinning an invisible Hula Hoop.

"Buying her a car is a good idea," I replied, snapping out of my trance and sticking to my manners. I really wanted to say, *Maybe I could buy that rusted piece of junk you keep up on cinder blocks in your front yard!* But I knew if Mom overheard me being rude I'd get instantly grounded and I wouldn't be able to go waterskiing.

"Don't let it happen again!" Miss Fry ordered. "Or else!"

I didn't want to know what she meant by "Or else." Miss Fry was a security guard at the high school. Once the mailman delivered her mail to our house by mistake and in with her letters there was something titled *SECUR-I-GARB: The Catalog Serving Security Professionals.* Inside were pictures of SWAT team outfits, knives, handcuffs, bulletproof vests, and lots more cool stuff. I wanted to keep it but Mom made me put it back on her front porch.

"It won't happen again," I replied as sweetly as possible to Miss Fry. I didn't want her to arrest me.

After she stormed off, Betsy yelled out from the kitchen, "Who was that?"

"Miss Fry," I yelled back. "She forgot to take her medication." The drugstore errand boy was always delivering little white bags to her door.

"That's not a nice thing to say," Betsy said.

"She threatened to do in Miss Kitty II," I explained.

"She's just a big talker," Betsy replied, and sneezed. "Don't listen to her."

"Hey," I asked, as I walked into the kitchen, "what are we having for dinner tonight?" Mom and Dad were going out to an Elks Club Halloween party and had given Betsy money for take-out food.

Betsy held up a coupon for a pizza. "I got it out of the newspaper," she said. "Halloween special. You can get two huge pizzas for the price of one, plus two free extra toppings each, plus they deliver."

"I want Hawaiian style," I said. "Pineapple and macadamia nuts with tuna."

Betsy raised her eyebrow. "That'll smell like puke—you'll have to eat that outside."

"I want hot-dog pizza," Pete said, "with sauerkraut."

"Believe it or not," Betsy said, "he's worse than you are."

Just then someone pounded on the door. "I'll get it," I yelled and pushed Pete to the floor. It was Tack.

"Get a move on," Tack said, panting. "My brother is ready to roll."

"In a lightning storm?"

"Yeah, and we have to carry golf clubs too," he said, grinning like a rotten-toothed pumpkin.

I knew Mom wouldn't let me go if I asked her, so I just hollered, "See you in a little bit," and ran out the door.

The thought of getting into a fast boat and skiing over jumps and doing flips and all sorts of stunts was pretty exciting. When I got into Jock's beat-up Impala convertible I asked, "What lake are we going to?"

Jock laughed. "You'll see," he said, and mashed down on the gas pedal. Just as the car lurched forward Miss Kitty II leapt through the window and onto my lap.

"Ouch!" I yelped as Miss Kitty II's claws dug into my thigh.

"Cool cat," Jock said, and whistled. Miss Kitty II climbed up onto his shoulder and stuck her head out the window as the car shot down the road.

I smiled. Miss Kitty II *was* a cool cat, and I could tell Jock liked me better already.

"About this skiing," Tack said. "We don't exactly have a boat."

"Then how do we ski?" I asked, confused.

"I'll show you," Jock said. "It's a little dangerous, but you'll get the hang of it just moments before you kill yourself."

Suddenly I lost my smile.

"Don't worry," he said. "It's Halloween. If you die this morning you can come back as a ghost in time to scare the pee out of someone tonight."

That didn't make me feel any better.

First, we pulled up onto an old dirt road that ran right next to a long straight canal. Jock opened the trunk and pulled out a plywood sled and about twenty yards of yellow nylon rope. He tied one end of the rope to the rear bumper of the car and attached the other to the sled. The sled was about two feet across and four feet long and had a rope handle in front so you could hang on. Jock showed me two rudder boards on the bottom of the sled and said we could steer it by shifting our weight to keep from sliding too far right or left and up onto the bank.

This was not my idea of skiing. I was thinking of all the sunny postcards with acrobatic bathing beauties stacked up in a pyramid, one on top of another as they effortlessly skied across Biscayne Bay. I took one look at the homemade sled full of splinters and said, "One of you guys go first. I'll watch and get the hang of it."

"I'll go," Tack said. He picked up the sled and heaved it into the canal. A black cloud of water bugs and mosquitoes took flight.

"Watch out for moccasins," Jock warned him.

I wished I had brought my snakebite kit.

Tack carefully worked his way down the bank and waded out into the water until he pulled himself up belly first onto the sled and grabbed the rope handle with both hands. "Okay!" he hollered. "Let 'er rip!"

I got into the seat next to Jock. Miss Kitty II had climbed onto the roof and dug her claws into the fabric of the convertible top like a streamlined furry ornament. Jock slowly drove forward until the rope was taut and then he hit the gas. The Impala took off with a roar and I turned around to watch Tack. He was kneeling and hanging on with both hands and zigzagging back and forth with a ragged rooster tail of water spraying out behind him. His hair was blown back and he had a flattened-out look on his face that seemed more like pain than pleasure. We went about a quarter of a mile until we got close to a rusty railroad bridge and Jock slowed down.

"Once I kept going," Jock said, "and when the rope

hit the top of the bridge it pulled the sled straight out of the water. Lucky for him Tack had already fallen off. The sled got caught in a trestle, and darn if the rope didn't pull the bumper clean off the back of my Dad's car."

I could just imagine my skull hitting one of the metal girders head-on at fifty miles per hour. At least I would be so dead that Dad couldn't kill me again for being hopelessly stupid.

Jock turned the car around and nodded at me. "You're on deck," he said. Then he laughed like a lunatic, and gunned the engine so that a cloud of gray smoke rose above us.

I pulled off my T-shirt. I was so pale my skin looked like the bloated bellies on the dead mullet that were floating upside down in the swampy water. My legs stuck out of the bottom of my baggy swim trunks like two pencils. I kept my sneakers on to protect my feet.

"Good luck," Tack said when he climbed up the bank. "It's a thrill ride is all I can say."

I stared down at the underbrush. I was certain there was a water moccasin just waiting to bite me.

"Hurry up," Jock said. "We haven't got all day. We have to get home and bloody up our houses and make our costumes for tonight."

I got up my courage and marched down the bank and into the dark water. I pulled myself up onto the sled and squatted as I took a good grip on the rope handle. Jock gave me the thumbs-up sign and slowly hit the gas, and when the line was taut he gunned it. I thought my arms were going to be yanked clean out of their sockets as the sled jolted forward. The steering was a mystery to me and before I could master it I was heading for the bank. Luckily the bank wasn't very steep, and somehow I went up over the bushes and was soon riding the sled down the slick, muddy road twenty yards directly behind the Impala. Jock was slowing the car down gradually, probably so I wouldn't end up eating his taillights. I was screaming and hanging on for my life when the Impala hit a little dip and Miss Kitty II flew up off the roof and rolled back over the top of the wet car, off the trunk, and landed in the middle of the road.

Oh my God, I thought. In a second I'm going to run her over with the sled and kill her.

But Miss Kitty was quick. I came at her as fast as a rocket and she jumped up and hit me in the face. I lost my grip and flew off the back of the sled and rolled into some bushes. When I looked up, Miss Kitty II was riding the sled right down the middle of the road.

I lurched forward and ran after them. Jock seemed to speed up for a while to give her a thrill. Finally he stopped. When I caught up to them Miss Kitty II jumped up into my arms and I gave her a big hug.

"Good cat," I said, and rubbed her head and ears.

"Very fine feline," Jock said knowingly. "She's something special."

"I'll trade you two regular cats for her," Tack said.

"Make it three," Jock added, shaking his head. "That cat is talented."

"No way," I replied. "Miss Kitty the Second and I are a team. I'm going to train her for the cat Olympics."

When I returned home I said to Betsy, "She's a genius cat. She's as smart as any trained dog, ever. She makes Lassie look like a yapping wig."

"Believe it or not," Betsy said. "Your cat may be from China. I read in the paper that the Chinese have figured out how to breed cats and dogs together and they have come up with a superhigh-I.Q. cat."

"I can believe it," I said, petting my hero.

"You better take care of that cat," Betsy advised me. "Once the government knows you have a Chinese hybrid they are going to take it and do what all to it in one of their secret pet laboratories."

"What labs?" I asked.

"You need to read the paper more," she said, and rolled her eyes at me. "The world is a lot bigger than this neighborhood."

I didn't have time to debate the size of the world—I was going over to Tack's house to help them decorate. I put Miss Kitty II on her dog-walking leash just in case the government came after her.

Tack and Jock were ready to decorate both their houses. Jock had me and Miss Kitty II lie down on the sidewalk as he drew dead body profiles around us with masking tape and then made bloodstains with cherry cough syrup. Tack was arranging the Slip 'N Slide down the front steps of one house. He had a box of ketchup packets he had collected from Burger King and scattered them on the front patio of the other house.

Suddenly the cops pulled up and one of them slowly got out. I thought maybe he was a government agent coming to take Miss Kitty II to a lab, so I hopped up and grabbed her leash.

"Howdy, boys," he said, then examined the sidewalk. "Nice art work. Very realistic. But it may be wasted. You do know that Halloween is canceled?"

"No way!" Tack hollered. "Who says?"

"Two murderers escaped from Rayford Prison, upstate, and jumped a train," he replied. "We had some agents board the train to flush 'em out and we think they may have jumped off around here. So, no trick-or-treating until those guys are captured. We don't want anyone to get spooked and shoot one of you kids."

"Wow," Tack said. "Cool."

That's probably what the newscaster was going to announce just before he got zapped by lightning, I thought.

"Is there a reward for 'em?" Jock asked.

"Yeah," the cop replied. "Automatic thousand dollars on any escaped prisoner. Well," the cop continued. "I know it stinks that Halloween is off, but help us out and don't roam the streets. We don't want to think that *you* are the convicts."

"I got a hunting rifle and if I see those guys, pow-pow-pow, I'm two grand richer," Jock said.

Yeah, I thought. Then you can buy a boat and some water skis.

The cop gave Jock a stern look. "No gun play," he said. "You just leave these guys to us. If you see anyone suspicious-looking, give us a call."

As soon as the police left we all ran around back to the tracks to see if we could find the prisoners.

"What do we do if the prisoners see us first?" I asked, feeling a bit nervous.

"Hide," Jock said.

I looked around. There was nothing but the tracks and gravel and sand. "Where?" I asked.

Jock smiled slyly. "I'll show you," he said. He walked over to a gap between two railroad ties. There was a hollowed-out space, like a shallow grave, big enough for one person to curl up in. "I dug it out myself," he said. "It's awesome. You just lie down in it and when the train comes it passes over your face and it is the most scared you will ever be in your life, but it's perfectly safe because you are lower than the tracks. Either of you guys want to do it?"

"Not me," I said. "That's insane."

"Come on," Jock said. "It's Halloween. If you don't get a good scare today you have to wait another whole year."

I didn't care if I had to wait a lifetime. I was not going to have a million-ton train just missing my head by inches. Our house had already been hit by lightning and I didn't want a train peeling my face off. Plus, I remembered what happened to Miss Kitty I. Her grave was not far away.

"I'll do it," Tack said. "This Halloween's a bust anyway and I could use a thrill." He curled up in the grave with his hands neatly folded over his chest and waited. Soon a train rumbled up the straightaway. Jock and I skipped down the gravel bank and watched as it roared over Tack.

After twenty-seven freight cars and a caboose passed we yelled out his name. But he didn't answer, and didn't get up. I feared the worst. We charged up the bank to where he was lying with his hands over his face. Blood was everywhere. We pulled his hands away and I expected to see a cracked-open skull and a bucket of fresh brain mush. Suddenly he popped up.

"Gotcha!" he howled, and threw a few empty ketchup packets at us.

I screamed bloody murder, then staggered away as if a dagger was in my belly. I was so scared I couldn't breathe. I held on to Miss Kitty II, sat down and put my head between my legs, and brayed like a donkey.

"I know you think you're scared now," Tack said, wiping the ketchup off his face with his shirttail. "But you got to get into that hole. I had my eyes open looking up at the bottom of the cars and then I peeked down the tracks, and there was this big old rusty chain hanging down hitting the ground and swinging back and forth and I thought if that thing hits me I'm d-e-a-d. But it just missed me. I could feel the breeze as it whizzed by like I was almost hit with a bullet. That close to death." He held his thumb and finger about a hair's width apart and stared between them. "Yep," he said reflectively, "I was this close to being a ghost."

"That's nothing," Jock said. "One time I was lying underneath a long, slow train, and I was tired of it, so I rolled out between the wheels. Man, if one of those things had caught me I'd be sliced in half like a fish."

I held Miss Kitty II even tighter. "Are you guys going to finish decorating?" I asked.

"Not me," Jock said. "What's the point? Nobody's going to be around to see it."

"I figure the only trick-or-treaters out tonight are the two convicts," Tack said. "I'm not going out there to become another murder victim."

"You got any good candy?" I asked.

"Naw," Tack replied. "The new mom is so cheap she's only handing out stale popcorn balls, and the old mom just gives away rotting fruit she gets cheap at the grocery store."

I stuck out my tongue. "Ugh," I said. "Come on, Miss Kitty II." We headed home.

Pete was dressed up as a plague-ridden flea. He had a floppy rubber mask covered with pussy boils. As soon as he saw Miss Kitty II he began to chase her around. "I'm a flea," he said in a Count Dracula accent. "I vant to suck your blood." Miss Kitty II jumped up on top of the refrigerator and hissed down at him.

"Hey, Dad," I said as he came in from the costume rental company. "Did you hear about the escaped convicts!"

"Shush," he said with a finger over his lips. He glanced over his shoulder. "Don't let your mom know. Betsy knows, and you can tell Pete after we leave. The last thing some convicts are going to do is hide out in a house full of kids. You'll be perfectly safe. Just keep the doors locked and the lights on."

He pulled out a two-part horse costume. "I got to the costume shop a bit late," he said, not at all happy. "They only had two-parters left. I got the horse, and I'll bet you dollars to doughnuts your mom is going to make me be the rear. But it could have been worse. The guy behind me had to rent the giraffe. Can you imagine, he'll have to carry his wife on his shoulders all night long." He smiled at the thought. "Now remember, don't go telling your mother about the escapees, or she won't go and the whole evening I'll have to sit around as a horse's rear end."

"Okay," I said.

But it was hard to keep my mouth shut. Each time Mom passed through the room I wanted to blurt out, "Escaped convicts are on the loose!" I knew Dad would kill me if I spilled the beans, so I went outside to the carport to fix my bike. The chain had come off the day before. We had been playing bicycle-horse polo. We didn't have horses or the right equipment so we used our bicycles and croquet mallets and one of the solid wooden balls. It was a good game unless you got hit with the ball, which hurt like something shot out of a pirate's cannon. That is what happened to my chain. Jock hit a low line drive right at me. I lifted my foot and the ball hit the chain and knocked it off the sprocket. Right after, Mom called me in for dinner, so I hadn't put the chain back on.

I was just threading it back onto the sprocket when Mom and Dad stepped out of the house.

"Have fun," Mom said, with the giant horse head under her arm. "Be extra nice to the little kids and don't eat too much candy or you'll never get to sleep."

"Sure," I replied as Dad jogged over toward me.

"Remember," he whispered, "keep the doors locked and don't open them no matter what."

"Don't worry," I whispered back, "we're not stupid."

He grunted and gave me a little swat with his tail.

As soon as the car left the driveway Betsy broke the news to Pete that Halloween was canceled.

"No big deal," he said. "Now we can split all our giveaway candy three ways."

After eating about a pound of chocolate bars I got so hyper from the sugar I dashed from window to window looking to find the escapees creeping through the bushes. Everyone had their porch lights on, but all the pumpkins were unlit. I plugged the TV back in just in case it fixed itself, but it only started to crackle again and smell like burnt rubber so I pulled the plug.

Finally Betsy came up to me. "I just ordered the pizzas," she said. "And I had them make up an extra-large Hawaiian puke pie just for you."

"That's really nice," I replied. I couldn't believe she actually ordered it for me.

"There is only one catch," she said, crossing her arms.

"What?" I asked.

"You have to go get it. The pizza place will make it, but they won't deliver to our neighborhood because of the escapees."

"No way," I said.

"Then I'll call them up and cancel," she threatened.

I loved pizza, and Hawaiian was my favorite. "Did you order extra pineapple and macadamia nuts?" I asked.

"Yes," she said. "Plus extra tuna and cheese."

That was too good to be true. "Okay," I said. "But if I'm not back in a half hour call the cops."

"I'll call the morgue first," she said, and stuffed the money into my jeans pocket.

"When I return," I said, opening the door, "I'll knock three times real fast, then two times real slow so you know it's me."

"Don't worry," she replied. "I'll smell you coming."

I picked Miss Kitty II up and carried her to my bicycle and placed her in the front basket. If I was going out on a mission to get pizza I wanted company. Plus she was tired of Pete trying to infect her with plague.

I figured the fastest way to get there was a straight line so I pedaled as hard as I could down the middle of our street. It seemed as if every dog in the neighborhood was searching for the prisoners. They barked insanely as I passed by. The shadows in the trees and brush flickered with life. Each gust rearranged their limbs, and their twiggy hands seemed to reach toward me as their leafy eyes followed mine. Radios and TVs were extra loud to let the convicts know people were home.

When I reached the main road I turned right under the streetlight and pedaled the three blocks up to Roy's Pizza Parlor. The Waffle House was farther down the street and I could see a few cop cars in the parking lot so I felt a lot safer.

I grabbed Miss Kitty II and ran inside the parlor. It smelled great.

"I'm here for the extra-large Hawaiian and whatever," I told the kid at the cash register.

"You mean extra-large broccoli? And a pepperoni and mushroom?"

"No," I said. "Hawaiian."

"Well, we only have one to-go order," he said, checking his ticket book. "Called in by Betsy Henry."

I knew she tricked me. Here I was, risking my life for a *broccoli* pizza. I was still staying away from red meat, but pizza was not the place to catch up on vegetables. "Well, could you put some pineapple and macadamia nuts on it?" I asked. "And tuna?"

"Why don't you just throw up on it yourself?" he said. He took it back to the kitchen. When he returned, I gave him the money.

"Be careful out there," he warned me. "One of our delivery drivers said two guys in striped uniforms tried to grab his door. One had a huge knife and tried to stab him. He was so freaked out we had to send him home."

"Okay," I replied. I clutched Miss Kitty II like a football under my left arm and balanced the pizzas with my right. I went outside, got her back in the basket, and held her down with the pizzas. Just as I sat on my bike I saw two cop cars speed out of the Waffle House parking lot. If they spotted me I was a goner. I pedaled really hard down the main street and was about a block away from home when I saw them. The two criminals. They were standing directly in the middle of the road. I hit my brakes and skidded to a stop.

"Hey," the big one yelled. His voice was muffled through a stocking he had pulled down over his face. "I smell pizza."

"I haven't had pizza since I was locked up for cold-blooded murder," said the other one.

I swung my bike around and just as I pressed down

on my pedal the chain snapped. I was dead meat. I hopped off my bike, grabbed Miss Kitty II and the pizzas, and headed between two houses. I reached the railroad tracks and ran down them, taking big jumping strides from one wooden tie to the next. When I looked over my shoulder the criminals were running behind me. All I could see were those black-and-white stripes as they yelled, "Pizza! Pizza, or death!"

I looked ahead to see if a train was coming around the far bend. No luck. I was about three houses from home but knew I'd never make it. The convicts were closing in behind me. I was desperate. So I did what I had to do. I ran toward the hole in the tracks. When I got to the space where Jock had dug the hole I threw myself facedown and lay on the pizza boxes. I held Miss Kitty II by my side.

"Lord, help me," I prayed, and closed my eyes. My pulse hammered. I held my breath. Miss Kitty II was spooked and clawed me but I didn't dare let her go.

"Hey, where'd he go?" one of the convicts asked.

"Don't know," the other said. I heard them turn and walk down the gravel bank.

After a while I peeked up over the rails. I didn't see them. My legs were all jelly so I crawled out of the hole. I stood and stumbled down the bank as I held Miss Kitty II and the pizzas. I was heading for home when a hand grabbed me from behind.

I whipped around. It was the murderers. "Don't kill

me," I hollered. "I'm just a kid. Take the pizzas. Just leave the cat alone."

"Got you good," Tack said, laughing as he pulled off his stocking mask.

"Yeah," Jock said. "I thought you were going to die of fright."

I dropped down to my knees. "What are you guys doing out?" I asked, panting. "The police said to stay at home."

"They caught the murderers already," Jock said.

"We just heard it on TV and ran outside and there you were."

"Well, I better get back home and tell Pete and Betsy. Our TV is broken and when kids start pounding on the door it will really flip them out."

"How about some pizza first?" Tack asked.

"Yeah," I said, still gathering my breath. "Take what you want."

He opened the broccoli-Hawaiian and sniffed. "Oh man," he groaned, "this thing is covered with barf chunks."

I sniffed it. "No way," I said. "It's Hawaiian."

"Yeah, Hawaiian barf," he said, and grabbed the other one. He flipped it open. "Pepperoni," he said happily. "Now we're talking American barf."

He took a slice and passed the pizza to Jock, who took two slices and made a sandwich out of them.

"Let's get going," Tack said, rolling the stocking back

down over his face, "while the element of surprise is on our side."

After they ran off I figured it was my turn to scare someone. And I knew exactly who I wanted to get.

I hustled over to Miss Fry's back porch. I peeked in her window to see if she was all dressed up in special police gear. But I didn't see anything. I squatted down and scratched at the bottom of her door.

"Heeelp meee. Saaave meee," I warbled. "The convicts got me and I'm bleeding to death." I stood up and began to back away from the door. I figured when she opened it I'd toss Miss Kitty II at her and see what happened.

Suddenly a hand grabbed the back of my collar and I fell over backward. I looked up. It was Miss Fry. She had snuck around on me.

"You smarmy little creep," she said. "You think I'm going to fall for your bozo tricks?"

"You're scaring me," I said.

She bent over and grabbed the front of my shirt. "Come into my house," she said, "and I'll really scare you! And your cat!"

I didn't know what else to do so I said, "Trick or treat."

"Treat," she replied, and grabbed the pizza boxes. She stepped over me and went in her back door. Then before I could scramble back up on my feet she threw the door open.

"Did you puke on this pizza?" she hollered.

"It's Hawaiian," I said.

She sniffed it. "Only a sick kid like you would eat garbage like this."

Then she threw it at me. I ducked and she slammed her door. Then one by one all her lights went off and she let out a bloodcurdling scream. I hope she takes her medication, I thought, as I crawled around her back yard sniffing toward my Hawaiian.

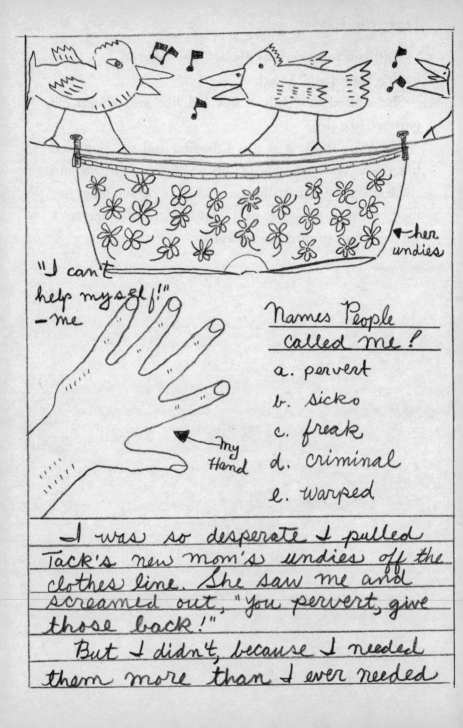

"I can't help myself!" —me

→ her undies

Names People called me!

a. pervert
b. sicko
c. freak
d. criminal
e. warped

→ My Hand

I was so desperate I pulled Tack's new mom's undies off the clothes line. She saw me and screamed out, "You pervert, give those back!"

But I didn't, because I needed them more than I ever needed

Bottom Line

I was hiding in the bushes wearing nothing but Tack's new mother's undies. They were baby blue with little white flowers and the elastic had gone saggy so I had to hold them up with one hand. I tried not to look at myself but every so often my eyes slipped, and when I caught a glimpse of my boy body squatting in the bushes wearing nothing but ladies' undies, I began to whimper like a hurt puppy.

I had been crying for over an hour and I was wondering just how long I was going to have to spend in the bushes. Even though south Florida didn't get too cold in the winter, it was still cool in the shade. I figured I'd wait until the sun went down before I made another run for the door and begged Betsy to let me in. Mom was working late at the bank and I wasn't sure what time Dad would return, when suddenly his car pulled into the driveway. Even before he had the engine turned off I sprang out of the bushes and thrust my head into his open window.

"Betsy made me do it!" I shouted. "It's all her fault! Honest! She locked me out of the house naked and I was desperate. You have to punish her." That's all I could say before I began to blubber again.

I must have surprised Dad. He jerked his head back and gave me a bug-eyed look. Then he cocked his fist behind his ear and got ready to pop me.

"Don't hit me," I pleaded, and covered my face. "I know I'm wearing ladies' underwear but I'm still your son."

"For God's sake," he cried in disbelief, and lowered his fist, "don't just stand there. Get into the car."

I ducked down and scurried around the front bumper before Tack's new mother spotted me again. She had caught me stealing the underwear off her clothesline and called me awful names and sent Jock out to find me and get them back. He had seen me slip into the bushes and all he did was stick his head in and say, "Don't worry, buddy. I won't tell Mom I found you. But take my advice and get some help."

"Thanks," was all I could reply.

I hopped into Dad's car and slouched way down in the seat like a common criminal. "Let's get out of here," I whispered.

Dad began to back out, then suddenly stopped. "Wait a minute. Don't you want to go into the house and get some clothes?"

"Can't I have your shirt?" I asked.

"No," he replied. "I don't have an undershirt on, and it would look pretty fishy if a shirtless adult was seen hanging around a boy wearing nothing but women's undies."

I lowered my head and pulled up on the slouching panties. My ears felt red and raw with shame.

"Now tell me," he asked, and turned the heater on. "Why is this all Betsy's fault?"

"Just drive around for a while so I can tell you my side of the story without Betsy butting in and twisting everything around," I requested.

"Okay. You can make a case for yourself now. And I'll be the judge as to who is right and wrong. But," he warned me, "you have to tell me the whole truth, and nothing but the truth. If you lie, I'll stop the car and make you walk home." Then he backed out into the road.

"It all started five days ago," I began, as he put the car in drive. "You know I haven't won an argument with Betsy in my entire life so I'm always waiting for her to show some kind of weakness. Last Monday I was walking down the hall when she stepped out of the bathroom with a huge pimple on her forehead. It had a pussy yellow head like a piece of candy corn and looked like a volcano just waiting to blow. I knew she had been operating on it because I could see the red nail marks around the base where she'd been squeezing. But she hadn't gotten it to pop. So when she passed by me I said, 'Hey, Cyclops. Got something stuck in your third eye?' And she just burst into tears and ran into her room. I thought she was faking me out until later, when I walked down the hall. I poked my head in her doorway. Her bed was covered with crushed-up tissues, and she was lying there with a pillow across her face as if she had suffocated herself. I told her I was sorry."

"Let me get this straight," Dad interrupted, peering down at me. "You were mean *first*, so at this point it looks like you started it."

"True," I said. "But you have to hear the rest and then you'll see that I'm the victim."

So while Dad continued to cruise up and down the tree-lined streets I continued talking. From my spot, crouched down next to the stereo, I sounded like an old radio drama. I used my hands as Jack and Betsy puppets and made bickering, yakking motions back and forth as I spoke.

"So Betsy sat up and looked at me with sad puppy eyes and said, 'We are brother and sister and should be nice to each other.' She was right and I felt even worse. Then she said, 'So, let's do something really important. Let's be kind and respectful toward each other for a whole week. Be supportive, and not one bit nasty.'

"I asked her if she was calling a truce. She said she wanted to set an example to the world that a brother and sister can exist in harmony under one roof.

"I said okay but asked what happens if one of us slips up and is nasty? She thought it over and said the punishment has to be severe, otherwise it would be too easy to slack off.

"I agreed. And we decided that the nasty person has to stand totally naked, buck naked, next to the tracks when the New England passenger train comes through. And we shook hands on it."

Dad pulled up to a red light and glanced down at me. "I'm getting a pretty good picture of what happened next," he said.

"Don't jump to conclusions," I cautioned. "Just hold your horses. Things started off really well," I said proudly. "That first day I was totally nice. I made her fresh-squeezed orange juice for breakfast. I cleaned the trash in her room. Took her overdue books back to the library and paid the fines. I mean, I was saintly *nice*. And she didn't even say thank you. Not once. On the second day I polished all of her shoes, cleaned out her fish tank, and crawled under her bed to find some missing earring backs. And still she didn't say thanks. Not only that, she didn't lift a finger to do one nice thing for me. But I was still trying. So on the third day I took all the little pieces of furniture and stuff out of her big Victorian dollhouse and repaired every piece. I Super-

Glued all the teeny-tiny handles back on the teacups, I rewove the loose threads in the Oriental rugs, and even touched up the royal portrait paintings on the walls. And still, she didn't say anything. On the fourth day I was running out of gas. I didn't do a thing for her. I wasn't nasty. I just didn't go out of my way to be nice."

"You know your sister was just setting you up," Dad said. "You *do* know that? She was just waiting for you to crack."

"Well, I didn't know that," I said reluctantly. "I was still trying to be a decent brother. So on the fifth day, to-day, I woke up and ironed all the clothes she had been putting off. And when I finished I said to her, 'Don't you think I've been a really good brother?' And she said, really snotty like, 'What do you want? A medal for being nice, when being nice is something that should come naturally and not be a special event?' And that hurt my feelings. And you know how I get. I started to redden up and snivel. And Betsy jumped all over me.

" 'Are you having an emotional emergency?' she asked.

"I said yes.

" 'Then I'm going to call 911 and ask for a psychologist,' she cracked.

" 'I don't need a shrink,' I yelled. 'I'm fine.'

" 'Well, if you are fine,' she replied, 'then *I* need a shrink.'

" 'I think you are being mean to me,' I said. 'We had a deal.'

" 'Since when,' she said as sweet as a sugar cube, 'is being concerned about my baby brother's mental health so mean?'

"Well, after she said all of that I didn't answer her, because I felt some ugly thoughts bubbling away in me and I knew if I stood there any longer with my mouth wide open horrid words would burst out and I'd lose the bet. So I stomped down to my room. And really, I tried to get my mind off Betsy. I started reading. I did some drawing in my diary, but my mind was not on my work. I had already slipped into a black mood and was planning my revenge. So I went into the back of my closet and that's when I got out my gallon jar of home-grown monster-sized roaches.

"I thought maybe eating a roach would bring her down to size. On the back of the biggest of them, with red nail polish I had painted *Zippy*. I plucked it out of the jar and stared it right in its shiny brown eyes. 'Okay, Zippy,' I said. 'You have been selected for a suicide mission. There is always a chance you might survive, but don't count on it.' Zippy didn't seem to mind. He just wiggled his inch-long antennae."

"Whoa," Dad said. "Did you do what I think you were planning to do?"

"You bet," I replied, and saw him smile, which made me think that he was definitely on my side and would pass judgment against Betsy. "Now imagine this," I said, getting really excited because this was the best part.

"The problem with getting a live roach into Betsy's

mouth while she napped was not getting the roach into her mouth, but getting it in without her knowing I did it. Because as soon as the roach started running around on her tongue her eyes would flip open, and if she saw me standing over her she would kill me on the spot then throw my dead, naked body across the train tracks. And she could do it, too. She has wrestled me down into the ground and made me eat dirt more than once. But I was about to avenge all the wrongs she had done me.

"I waited until she went into her room to take a nap. I stood outside until she was sound asleep. Then I cracked open her door a few inches to where I had a good view of her. I had to wait until she was on her back.

"While I waited, I got ready. In one hand I had your 25-foot, spring-loaded, self-retractable tape measure. In the other hand I had Zippy. In the kitchen I had squeezed a drop of honey onto the tip of the metal tape, and when I put Zippy on he got busy slurping. And then my moment arrived. Betsy rolled over onto her back and her mouth opened into a beautiful round target. I pulled the stiff metal tape out of the case, keeping the tension just right so that the tape didn't snap down and knock Betsy in the head. Zippy was busy with the tiny drop of honey and stayed right out on the tip as I pulled out more and more tape.

"Finally, I was ready. From where I was standing, it

seemed to me that Zippy was directly over her mouth. I counted to three and then slowly turned the tape sideways. Just as Zippy lost his grip and slid down into her mouth, I released the lock on the tape and it snapped back into the case. As she screamed out loud I was already three steps down the hall and ducking into the coat closet.

"I stood there in the dark listening to her. First there was the scream, then the spitting, then I could hear a shoe hit the floor. It *was* a suicide mission for Zippy. Then I heard her in the bathroom brushing her teeth, then gargling, then taking a shower."

I looked up at Dad to see if he thought it was as wonderful as I did. He was making a gruesome face and smacking his lips as if he had just swallowed a roach.

"My God," he said, "what did she do next?"

"She stomped down to the living room and made an announcement. 'I just want you to know,' she hollered, 'whoever you are, and I have a good idea who you are, that I don't believe for a minute that a roach named Zippy just fell into my mouth by accident.'

"Suddenly my desire for revenge was replaced with fear for my life. I knew what I had done was wrong. I knew that I should just apologize to Betsy and beg for mercy. But I also knew that it was too late. She wouldn't forgive me and in no time I'd be standing naked next to the tracks. So I figured I'd try a new strategy. I hid out for a while then went into her room. She was sitting on her bed. 'I'm going down to the store,' I said as nice as possible. 'Anything I can get for you?'

" 'Yes,' she said. 'It's my turn to empty out the cat box and I need some fresh litter. Will you get some?'

" 'You bet,' I said. And when I left her room I thought she wasn't mad at me at all and didn't seem to blame me for the roach in her mouth. I figured I had gotten away with it and was in a pretty good mood now that I had released some revenge from my system. When I came back Betsy was by the kitchen back door next to the litter box. I handed her the ten-pound bag of litter and she smiled at me and then threw it down onto my foot. Then, as I hopped up and down, she twisted her fingers in my hair and jerked me forward. I fell over and she held my face just above the cat box. It was supposed to be self-cleaning but it still stank.

" 'I know you put the roach in my mouth. Now, confess or else.'

" 'Or else what?' I said desperately.

"She lowered my face further. 'Or else I'll make you eat dinner right now.' She dredged my face back and forth across the litter until I confessed. I told her I only did it because I was being so nice to her and she didn't even say thank you.

" 'Is that the only reason you are nice?' she said. 'Are you only searching for a good-puppy pat on the head?'

"I said it's good manners to return the favor when someone does something nice for you.

" 'It's good manners to always honor your bets,' she replied. 'Now get naked. And wipe the litter off your lips.' She looked at the kitchen clock. 'The passenger train will be here in fifteen minutes and you better get ready to put on a show.'

"I went into the bathroom and undressed. When I came out, the back door was wide open.

"Betsy hollered, 'To the tracks!' and I ran directly for the toolshed, but it was locked. Then I ran a little farther and hugged the rubber tree. I reached up and grabbed a low branch and ripped it from the trunk. I held the thick, wide leaves against my privates and ran screaming toward the tracks. I got over the fence and climbed the gravel bank and stood there, waiting. I kept looking back at the house and hoping you would come home and rescue me, but you didn't. Then, in a few minutes the passenger train rounded the bend to the north and headed toward me. I just stood there looking up at the windows filled with people. I figured the only fun I would get out of this whole deal was watching the look of surprise on their faces. With one hand I held the rubber plant leaves in place and with the other I waved as I did a little hula dance. Some people were shocked, others smiled, some looked really confused.

"After the train passed I ran directly back to the house. I tried to open the back door but it was locked. I desperately ran around to the front door. It was locked too. And all the windows were shut and locked. I returned to the back of the house. 'Let me in,' I hollered, and beat on the door. Betsy cracked open a window. She said I'd cheated and had to wait for the next passenger train to make up for my violation of our agreement.

"The next train was in four hours. I must have gone a little nuts," I said, trying to get Dad's sympathy on a temporary-insanity plea. "I needed to find some clothes. I looked over at Tack's house and saw some things on their clothesline. I made a mad dash across our back yard to theirs. I was almost to their clothesline when the new Mrs. Smith opened her back door and started yelling at me. She called me indecent and said to go put some clothes on. So I did.

"I grabbed the first thing I could reach off her line and ran. As it turns out, I grabbed her undies, and as I hopped away on one foot while getting my other through the leg hole, she yelled out, 'Pervert!'

" 'I'm not a pervert,' I yelled. 'I'm just naked.' "

I turned toward Dad and delivered my final defense: "By then I had both my legs in the panties and I ran off and hid in the bushes and that's when Jock came looking for me and now you know everything. So, don't you think Betsy was wrong for what she did and should be punished?"

"I suppose you want some justice?" he said.

"Exactly," I replied, relieved that he knew what I was going through. "I'm tired of being on the low end of the totem pole."

"I'm thirsty," Dad said. "Let's go to the drive-through and get something to drink and that will give me time to sort this out and come up with a verdict."

"Okay," I said, a little disappointed that he didn't immediately see that I was the injured party in this case.

After we got our drinks Dad finished about half of his before he pulled over by the side of the road. "Well," he said gravely, "here is what I think. First, I'm disappointed that my oldest son is exposing himself to innocent people on trains and then running around the neighborhood dressed in women's underwear."

"I just told you," I said, pleading. "It's not all my fault. I'm the victim."

"Being or not being the victim is not the point in this case," he stressed. "If you want to be known as a serious person on this planet you have to draw the line somewhere with what you *will* or *will not* do. And wearing women's underwear around the neighborhood is way, way below that line."

"But she locked me out of the house," I reminded him. "I was desperate."

"That's not the point," he said again. "So let me restate the point so you never forget it. In *life* you set high standards for yourself. You live by those standards and you never sink below them. *This* is the bottom line. And this is how you can judge for yourself your own behavior. Because if you can't make good judgments for yourself, nobody is going to do the job for you, especially Betsy."

I pursed my lips and lowered my head for his sentencing.

"Didn't you think it was wrong to be mean to your sister?" he asked.

"Yes, sir," I said.

"Didn't you think it was wrong to drop a pet roach into her mouth?"

"Oh, yes, sir," I said.

"Didn't you think it was dumb to stand naked in front of a train?" he asked.

"Yes, sir," I replied.

"And didn't you think it was even dumber to put on the neighbor lady's undies?"

"Yes, sir."

"Since I have judged against you in this case do you have anything to say for yourself?" he asked.

"No, sir," I said.

"You must apologize to your sister for your mean behavior, and you must apologize to the new Mrs. Smith for running off in her underwear, and you must promise me you will never do it again."

"Yes, sir. I promise not to wear ladies' undies again."

"Then this case is closed," he announced, and pounded on the dashboard with his fist as if it were a judge's gavel.

On the way home I thought about the point Dad had

made, and he was right. I wasn't mad at him at all. I was guilty as charged. I had behaved lower than the standards I had set for myself. I had let Betsy get to me, and once more, I was the sucker. But I had learned my lesson, and I never again wanted to slip below the bottom line.

That night I apologized to Betsy, and after dinner I went back to my room. I climbed out my window and snuck around to the Smiths' clothesline. I pinned the big undies back onto the line. They were wet because I had sprayed them off with the garden hose. Also pinned to the undies was my apology: I'M SORRY I BORROWED YOUR UNDIES AT A TIME WHEN I WAS UNDER EXTREME EMOTIONAL STRESS. PLEASE DON'T MENTION THIS TO ANYONE AND I PROMISE YOU IT WILL NEVER HAPPEN AGAIN. JACK HENRY.

After I cried in Tack's basement I went home. But I couldn't stop crying, so finally I went into the shower and with the water running down my face I cried as much as I wanted.

Crybaby

I was sitting on the floor with a book in the far corner of my bedroom. The wide pine planks were splintered from wear so I had a small round piece of linoleum to sit on. It was the fleshy color of a slice of baloney with odd white flecks which I imagined were chunks of pork brain, and black flecks which I imagined were rotten teeth. It made me a little ill to sit on it because I was still a vegetarian. But it was better than sitting on splinters.

There was just enough dim reading light coming through the curtains and I wanted it this way. I wasn't thinking about my eyes. I was reading *A Day No Pigs Would Die* and the father and Robert had just slaughtered Pinky the pig on a cold winter morning. The father had taken a crowbar and crushed Pinky's skull, and then slit her throat with a curved knife, and the blood drained into the fresh snow. It was so sad the tears were streaming down my face and soaking the neck on my T-shirt. I had read the same book over and over, and each time I reached the killing part I couldn't stop myself from crying.

And that was the whole point. To feel so sad, so completely sad, and to cry so much that when I finished the book there would be fewer tears inside me and I might feel more like a man. I would feel tougher and drained of sadness like Robert felt after his pig was killed. But although I could feel as sad as Robert, I could never seem to feel as much of a man. And so I kept crying.

Suddenly Betsy pushed my bedroom door open and flicked on the blinding overhead light. Before I could wipe away the tears she saw me hunched down in the corner, bingeing on my sad thoughts.

"What are you reading?" she snapped. "Your pathetic autobiography?"

She leapt at me and snatched the book out of my hand. "*A Day No Pigs Would Die,*" she scoffed. "What'd you do. Get a pardon?"

I stood up but before I could clear my eyes and fight back she grabbed the soft band of fat above my hips with both her hands and swung me around. "Hey, Pete!" she yelled. "Hey, get in here!"

She was killing me. I knew she wanted Pete to grab

the fat above my other hip and they would have a tug-of-war which she called the "Battle of the Bulge."

"Let me go," I yelped.

"Crybaby," she said, and twisted my fat as if it were the key on a windup toy. I danced up and down on my tiptoes like a spastic string puppet. "You're the most girlie boy I've ever met. You aren't on a baseball team. You're not a Boy Scout. You hang out at the library. You even collect stamps."

"I don't play with dolls," I shouted back.

"You should," she replied, and pushed me to the floor. My lower lip quivered and I began to blubber. "Look at you," she said with contempt. "If something really tragic happened you'd be in deep doo-doo."

I sprang forward. If I were a bull I would have gored her. But she dodged me. I ran from my room, slamming directly into Pete. I pushed him out of the way, then tripped over Miss Kitty II. "Sorry, sorry, sorry," I said as I crawled down the hall on my hands and knees.

"Oink, oink, oink," Betsy hollered behind me.

I jumped up and dashed out the kitchen door. I kept going across the back yard and up over the fence until I reached the railroad tracks. Then I sat there, right in the middle of the hot tracks with my chin on my knees, waiting for the train to run me down. I told myself I didn't care if I was flattened like all the pennies and frogs and Coke cans I had set on the rails. I didn't care if my blood and guts greased the wheels. I didn't care if everyone I had ever loved cried when they heard I was dead. I wanted to be hard and cold and unfeeling and manly and able to bear awful tragedies like smashing in a pet pig's skull and slitting its throat. If I couldn't be callous and hard-hearted, I didn't want to live.

But I wasn't anything at all like what I wanted to be. When I watched tearjerker movies, I cried. When I listened to sad ballads, I cried. When I saw roadkill, I cried. When I passed the Miss Kitty grave, I cried. When I read awful newspaper stories about adults who beat up kids, I cried a lot. It's a wonder I didn't have ugly, brown tearstains running down my cheeks like I always noticed on little white lapdogs.

And each time a glassy tear slipped out of my eye it seemed that Betsy caught me. She called me a crybaby, a wimp, a candy butt, a sissy, a pantywaist, a sniveler, and a mama's boy.

One night, while I rubbed Mom's tired legs, I asked her about my crying problem. She said I was just going through a sensitive stage. "You'll get older and wiser and tougher and put the world in perspective," she said. "You used to cry over spilt milk when you were two, now you don't. So, don't worry, you'll move on."

I felt awful when she said I'd move on because the other night at dinner I spilled my milk and felt like a baby and had to jump up from the table and get a kitchen cloth just so nobody could see the tears welling up in my eyes.

Well, I was going to change my crying ways. I was going to toughen up and learn how to be hard and solid and unshakable like a man. Real men didn't cry, they stood up to danger.

I saw a train come around the bend and felt the rail tie tremble from the weight of it, but I didn't budge. The expression on the face of the engine was uncaring. Two black windows stared out above a rust-pocked flat front and a grill of metal bars. It could roll over me and never flinch. When it was only a hundred yards away I held my ground. Fifty yards away and the stones around my feet began to jiggle like popcorn popping. A lion's mane of heat buckled the air around the engine. I didn't move. Twenty-five yards away and the engineer pulled the cord on his air horn. The sudden blast unnerved me and I screamed as loud as I could and dove headfirst off the tracks and tumbled down the gravel bank with my hands over my face. I kept screaming but couldn't hear myself over the throbbing drone of the engine and clacking wheels. Finally, I tried to play as if I were dead, but the gravel was so sharp I couldn't imagine heaven as anything more than a bed of nails.

After the train passed I hopped up and went over to Tack's original house. I felt tougher already. I was bruised and bleeding along a few scratches but I wasn't crying about it. I knocked on his door and while I waited I took a stick I found on the ground and jabbed it at one of my cuts. It hurt, and my eyes glazed over, but still no tears. Maybe I was getting tougher, I thought, yet I knew the ultimate test was before me.

When Tack opened the door I jumped inside. They had air-conditioning now and if the door was open longer than two seconds his new mom pitched a hissy fit and yelled at us for letting the cold air escape.

"I have a favor to ask you," I whispered.

"You can't give back the cat," he said. "Too late."

"It's not about the cat," I replied. "I love the cat. Take me to your basement. I need to see the spot again."

He was silent for a moment. "Haven't you had enough?" he asked.

"I'm tougher this time," I said. "I can handle it."

"No you can't," he said. "Nobody, not even Jock, can handle the spot without . . ."

"Don't say it," I said, cutting him off. "I don't want to hear the c-word."

He turned and I followed him around to the kitchen, where he opened a door that looked like it might be a closet, only there were steps that led down into the basement. Tack flicked on the lights.

"You go. I'm staying up here," he said.

I forced myself down the stairs. At the bottom I

walked over to the far side of the pool table. The balls were spread out across the green felt where a game had suddenly stopped. Each ball had a fuzzy cap of dust on it. There, on the floor, on the smooth, pearly gray concrete, was a drawing of a cross and the words JIMMY SMITH. GONE BUT NOT FORGOTTEN. LOVED BY ALL. I stood over the cross and took a deep breath. I gritted my teeth and stared down at the painted memorial and recalled the story. One night while playing pool with his buddies, Tack's oldest brother, Jimmy, had opened a bottle of whiskey and drank it straight down like water. He set the bottle on the edge of the pool table, and then his eyes rolled back and he collapsed into a heap on the floor. He died instantly from alcohol poisoning.

It was about the saddest story I had ever heard, and I stood there and looked at the cross, then read the inscription. I knew that if I was going to be a man I was supposed to buck up and not cry. But I didn't stand a chance, and within seconds the tears streamed down my face and left dark drops on the dusty floor. I sniffed and glanced up to see Tack standing next to me. He was sobbing, and that really got me going.

"Tell me again why he did it," I said after a few minutes.

"Mom said he was a sensitive soul in an ugly, cruel world. But I read his diary. He said he was depressed and had a death wish."

"Why'd he want to die?" I asked, already knowing the answer.

"Because," Tack said gravely, "he was sick and tired of feeling sad all the time."

My knees buckled when he said that. I knew exactly how Jimmy Smith felt, which only sent a fresh wave of tears rushing down my face.

"It's just so sad," Tack said, wiping his eyes on the tail of his shirt. "I can't come down here without crying."

"I know what you mean," I said. Then suddenly I felt confused because both of us, two boys, were standing side by side and crying. It seemed as forbidden as if we were smoking cigarettes, or kissing. I knew if Betsy peeked through one of the narrow, ground-level basement windows and saw us down here, she would think we were sick and needed to be put into an insane asylum. And maybe she was right. Or maybe she was wrong. Because if it was okay to cry, then Tack was the greatest friend I ever had. But if all this crying was warped, then Tack was a bad influence and I should stay away from him. I didn't know which. "Let's get out of here," I said, and he agreed.

"Hey, Tack," I said when we had shut the door behind us and were standing in the kitchen, sniffling. "Have you ever punched anyone really hard?"

"Yeah," he replied. "Why?"

"Punch me," I said, and jutted out my chin. "In the face."

"Why?"

"I need to toughen up," I said.

"Look," Tack said. "If you want to toughen up, you need to suck it up. You don't need to take a sucker punch."

"Well, maybe you're right," I said, thinking that he *was* a great friend.

"Tell you what," he suggested. "Come with me to my Boy Scout meeting tonight. We're looking for new members. It's just guys, and we'll eat beans and sleep out in tents and cut deadly farts with the flaps closed and you'll feel better."

I remembered what Betsy had said about me not even being a Boy Scout, so I said yes, even though I had no real interest in smelling someone else's gas.

That night I got off to a bad start. At the cookout I was afraid to tell all the scouts I was a vegetarian, so I took my two hot dogs and when no one was looking I fed them to the scoutmaster's big dog. After that it kept following me around. I ate the hot-dog rolls loaded up with ketchup. Each time I took a bite the ketchup gushed out and smeared my face, so I looked like a cannibal.

When dinner was over we sat in a circle around a campfire. I wished we were in the woods instead of the scoutmaster's back yard. I stared into the flames and thought about Indian gurus who could walk on hot coals. It's all mind over matter, I said to myself. The same with crying. It's all mind over matter. I just had to practice. I gave myself a crying test by thinking of sad images—a dog with a broken leg, a starving child, a war hero's return to his family.

Before I could cry Tack leaned over and whispered in my ear. "Whatever you do," he said, "don't laugh at the scoutmaster's name."

Just then the scoutmaster stood up. He was thin but very muscular and wore a green uniform studded with colorful badges. "Let me introduce myself in case I haven't met all the newcomers yet," he announced. "My name is Sunny Winterbottom." I tried to hold back a laugh but it snorted out through my nose. I just couldn't help myself, and after I snorted I bent over cackling. I pulled the neck of my T-shirt up over my head, and the bottom out over my knees and laughed down into my belly like a sputtering lunatic tied up in a sack. And every time Tack jabbed me with his elbow and begged for me to be quiet I just let out another howl.

Sunny Winterbottom seemed to know why I was laughing. "Young man," he commanded, "stand up." When I peeked back up through the neck of my shirt he was pointing at me.

I stood and looked around. Everyone was staring back at me. I didn't know any of them.

"Our troop is called the Wolf Pack and we don't make

fun of each other. We believe, like a pack, that we should stick together, fight for one another, hunt together, eat together, and bond together until death."

I glanced down at Tack. He slowly shook his head back and forth. "I warned you," he mouthed.

No sooner had he said that than I felt my face redden and the tears well up in my eyes. *Don't cry, don't cry, don't cry,* I scolded myself. Don't you *dare* cry in front of Tack's manly friends. I gritted my teeth and fought back. I concentrated on an image of the Dutch boy with his finger plugging up a dike filled with tears, and slowly I felt my tears recede.

"Now," Sunny Winterbottom said to me, "tell us a story about how you expressed your manhood through the spirit of the wolf."

I wasn't sure what he meant, and for a moment I wondered if he wanted me to say that I peed on car tires, dug up bones in the back yard, chased rabbits, and howled at the moon.

"A story," he explained. "Where you did something *manly.*"

"Okay," I said, trying to think quickly. "We had a vicious house cat that was always eating mice and so I put a bell around its neck and saved the mice but then the cat got hit by a train because the bell was so heavy it couldn't get off the tracks in time."

"Well, where is the *manly* part to the story?" Sunny Winterbottom asked.

"Saving the mice," I replied, as my voice began to quiver.

Tack raised his hand before I slipped into a crying fit. "Mr. Winterbottom, sir," he said. "The cat was an evil killer."

Everyone cracked up, which gave me a chance to flick away a few stray tears. Then I sat down and listened as the other kids told incredible tales of calling on the spirit of the wolf to help them shoot deer, skin alligators, survive boat sinkings, catch thieves, and win sports events. The whole time I sat there thinking that I was nothing but a pathetic crybaby.

After a session of arm wrestling, knot tieing, and edible-bug identification, it was time for bed. Mr. Winterbottom called me to his side. "I think you need some extra muscle," he said. "You get to sleep with the mascot in your tent. The spirit of the wolf dog will enter your body during the night and in the morning you will be one of us." He punched me on the shoulder and I stumbled away.

I crawled inside the tent. The dog was happy to follow because I had fed him earlier. Sunny lowered the flap and slapped the canvas roof. "Good night," he said. "Sleep tight, and open your soul to the spirit of the wolf dog." I could only think of the movie *The Wolf Man* and figured by the morning I would have fangs and hair all over my face and body and live in fear of a full moon.

The dog was huge. It took up half the tent. The air was hot and humid so I slept on top of my sleeping bag and the dog slept against me. It was a very friendly dog and in the morning it licked my face and woke me up and I thought, Well maybe the spirit of the wolf has entered me and I've toughened up.

I crawled out of the tent and went to the bathroom, which was in Sunny Winterbottom's basement. There was a hazy mirror over the toilet and as I peed I glanced at myself. My hair was dirty and spread all over my head like swoopy icing on a cupcake. I didn't look any more manly except for huge purplish spots all over my face and neck. Seeing them gave me a bad feeling. I reached up and touched one that was on the corner above my eyelid. It was something soft, like a warm raisin stuck to my skin. I began to pull on it but it wouldn't come off. It was as if I was trying to pull a sandbur off of a sock. Finally it tore away and left a smudge of fresh blood where it had been attached. I held the purple thing in my hand and looked into its tiny red face. "Oh my God," I cried out, "I'm covered with ticks!"

They were everywhere. I yanked another off from beneath my chin, and another from inside my ear. The dog must have had ticks, I thought, and now I have the spirit of the ticks. I lifted my shirt. There was one in my belly button. I didn't dare look any lower. I turned and ran out of the bathroom. The tears were streaming down my face. I didn't say goodbye to anyone. I hopped on my bike and raced for home. I could barely see with the tears in my eyes, but I didn't care if I ran head-on into a tree and died.

When I got to the front yard Betsy was outside picking up the morning paper. I pulled my bike up next to her. I was sobbing and didn't care what she thought of me. "I'm covered with ticks," I said, hysterical and desperate. My arms flapped up and down as if I were on fire. "Help me."

"Relax," she said. "You're overreacting. Go around to the shed and strip down. I'll meet you there."

I did, and took off everything but my underwear. While I waited for Betsy I checked my privates. I didn't find anything. Betsy arrived with a pair of tweezers, rubbing alcohol, a book of matches, and a candle. "This is how we'd take care of ticks when I was in the Girl Scouts," she explained matter-of-factly.

"This happened to you?" I asked.

She tweezed a plump tick from my eyebrow and held it over the flame of the candle. It swelled up then popped, and the blood sizzled like grease on the grill.

"If you sleep outdoors with animals it's bound to happen," she said. "No big deal. We used to have contests to see who had the most ticks. We'd line them up on the ground and squish them with our thumbs and they'd pop and we'd measure to see which one squirted blood the farthest."

"Didn't they make you cry?" I asked.

"No," she said. "They are just *ticks*. No big deal. You pull them off, burn them, and go on your merry way. You're just a crybaby is all. Even girls don't get worked up over a few little ticks."

"I think I lost a lot of blood," I whimpered. "The ticks drained me. I feel weak." I leaned back against the rung of a ladder. I touched my forehead to check if I was running a fever.

"I hope you don't talk to your friends like this," Betsy said. "Or you won't have any."

I didn't dare tell her about Tack and me crying together over his brother's death spot. She'd never understand.

When she finished she closed her eyes and made me take off my underwear and wrap a clean towel around myself. "Go take a hot shower and pull yourself together," she said, exhaling with disgust. "If something really bad happens you're going to be a wreck."

After my shower I returned to my room. I unlocked my diary and it sprang open to the page where I kept the flattened cowbell for a bookmark. All I could think about was death and Jimmy Smith and I didn't write a word. Instead, I cried all over the pages, and the paper puckered up as if it had bee stings all over. I snuggled across my bed with Miss Kitty II. As I rubbed her soft fur I kept feeling her skin for ticks but only found small clumps of dirt. I was still so upset, all my muscles twitched and tightened with cramps and I felt stiff all over as if I were slowly turning into plaster. I began to think about all those petrified Romans that were dug up at Pompeii. I had seen pictures of them in a book of ancient Italian ruins. There were people in the act of eating or working or doing hundreds of normal things that people do every day when suddenly they were entombed forever from the shower of lava and ash of Mt. Vesuvius. I thought that if I were suddenly solidified forever, right at this exact moment in time, people would someday dig me up and put me in a museum. A sign around my neck would read: A SAD, SAD BOY OF THE LATE 20TH CENTURY. Viewers would stare at my face and say, No wonder this kid didn't survive. He was just lying around, hugging his kitty, crying, and feeling sorry for himself.

I felt miserable and needed to pulled myself together. When Dad had a tough day he had a drink. That was a man's approach and maybe it would work for me too, I thought. I hopped out of bed, opened the door, and peeked down the hallway. No one was in sight. I heard Betsy in her room practicing ballet leaps from one side of her rug to the other. The entire house shook as if being struck with a battering ram. Pete was down at the Tiny Bubbles indoor pool with Mom. Dad was out playing golf with a construction tycoon.

"It's now or never," I said to myself. I bent over like a sneak thief, dashed into the kitchen, and opened the cabinet over the toaster. This is where Mom kept the cooking sherry. I figured it would do the trick. I grabbed the brown bottle, shoved it under my shirt, and hustled back to my room. Mom would not allow me to lock my bedroom door, because she said she never knew what I was "up to." She was right to worry. I went into my closet and pulled the door tight. There was no light except from the crack under the door. I set the bottle down between my feet and turned the screw top. I lifted the bottle to my lips. Then I took a big breath and began to swallow in big, long gulps like a giant drinking the entire ocean. But the sherry would not go down my throat. It pooled in my mouth and boiled like molten lava until suddenly it erupted and I spewed it out all over my clothes. Tears from the burn of it in my throat ran down my face. I tried again to swallow the sherry but could only manage to get a trickle down. Finally, I made one last effort. I held my nose and drank whole mouthfuls, then set the bottle back on the floor.

In a moment I felt a little sick and dizzy, and afraid of what I had done. "Oh my God," I suddenly cried out, "I'm going to die like Jimmy Smith and I don't want to."

I recalled the hand-painted cross and inscription on Tack's basement floor—JIMMY SMITH. GONE BUT NOT FORGOTTEN. LOVED BY ALL. I imagined my own inscription—JACK HENRY. DROWNED IN A RIVER OF HIS OWN HOT TEARS. Maybe Mom and Dad and Betsy and Pete picked on me too much. Maybe I was a crybaby. But it wasn't worth dying for.

I jumped up and ran from my closet and into the utility room. "I need to pump my stomach," I muttered. "I want to live." I plugged in the vacuum cleaner and stuck the rubber hose in my mouth. I flicked on the switch and sealed my lips around the nozzle. The pull of the vacuum took my breath away. I felt my lungs quiver like leaves in a hurricane. My tongue flickered like a neon flame. But nothing came up out of my stomach.

I turned off the switch and took a deep breath.

Maybe the sherry was having a different effect over me. I no longer felt like a crybaby. Instead, I felt tough. Saving my own life was making me feel better already. I ran outside. The sun was blinding. The sky was polished with bright light. The electric buzz of heat made everything seem even more alive. I felt powerful and manly as I marched toward the tracks.

I was heading for Tack's shallow hole between the railroad ties. He liked to lie down in it and let the trains pass over his body. He had called me a chicken because I wouldn't try it. Now, it didn't seem so dangerous. I lay down in the hole with my hands folded behind the back of my head. I closed my eyes and waited. I was so still bugs walked across my face. Before long the earth began to vibrate. I heard the wheels screech as the train turned the bend before coming my way. The ground began to jump, then a rush of hot air roared over me. I opened my eyes wide and watched the tons of speeding black metal pass a foot above my face. I knew that if I really wanted to die I just had to lift my head and, faster than a guillotine, I'd have it chopped off.

After the train passed I hopped up and dusted myself off, then walked down to the Kellys' house. They had a mean pit bull on a chain that scared the life out of me each time I passed it. But not anymore. I stood on the other side of the road and flung frangipani pods at it. Each time I hit him, he growled and bared his teeth. "Ha, ha, ha," I laughed like a robot as I walked toward him. "You are a mean dog, but I am meaner." He tugged at his chain, his eyes glazing over with pure hatred. "Can't get me, can you? You'd like to. You'd love to. You'd love to hurt me, bite me." I stretched my neck way out. "Bet you'd like to get your teeth on this," I said, and poked at my throat. "But you can't, because you are chained up. Ha!"

He was foaming at the mouth and drooling and snapping his killer jaws at me as I turned and marched off in a goose step like a German soldier.

I went back home and got the ladder out of the shed and propped it against the wall. I climbed up and hoisted myself onto the tin roof. I looked down at the ground. It was hard. But I was harder. I closed my eyes and dove off like Superman. I hit the ground with a thud. It felt as if an elephant had stepped on my chest.

Air hissed out of my mouth. But I didn't cry. I picked myself up and went into the house.

Betsy was taking a shower. I quietly pushed the bathroom door open. She was singing a song from *Madame Butterfly*. I wanted to sing along in a goofy voice but instead reached out and flushed the toilet.

"Eiiii," she wailed as a full blast of hot water zapped her on the back. She whipped open the curtain and wrapped it around herself.

"You!" she hollered furiously. "Are a dead man."

"Bring it on," I said, motioning her toward me with my hands. "Come on. Hit me with your best shot."

"I don't know what's gotten into you," she said, waving her fist at my face. "But you just wait! When you least expect it—wham! And you'll be tick juice."

"Oh, you scare me," I said sarcastically, and walked away. I didn't feel scared at all. In fact, I felt sleepy. I went into my bedroom and sat on my bed. "I'm cured," I thought. "No more crying for me. A little tough-guy practice and suddenly I'm the baddest bear in the forest." Miss Kitty II jumped up on my lap looking for me to pet her. "No way," I said. "You are out of here. I don't need cat love." I picked her up and dropped her out the open window. "Sleep on the cold ground and toughen up," I shouted at her. "That'll fix you."

I threw myself back across my bed and thought, If Vesuvius blew up now I'd be captured forever with a

snarl on my face. In a museum I'd be wearing a sign
that read: TOUGH GUY FROM THE 20TH CENTURY. People
would look at me and think, "Gee, I wish that great guy
had survived."

When I woke up in the morning my chest was sore
and bruised. I touched one of my ribs and winced. The
pain felt manly. I had slept in my clothes so I just
walked out to the kitchen.

"Hey, buddy," Dad said. "Why don't you come with
me this morning. I have to deliver some beams. I'll let
you work the levers that raise and lower the truck bed.
Then we can go get a big Italian sub and I'll bring you
back home. How about it?"

"Sure," I said. "Some hard work will do me good." I
grabbed a piece of toast and followed Dad out of the
house across the cracked flagstone walkway. I climbed
up onto the metal truck step and opened the door on
the cab and got in.

Dad pulled the choke back on the engine, turned the
key, and pumped the gas pedal. We just heard, "Whack-
a-whack-a-whack-a-whack-a-YOWL!" and then a few
more cat screams before the roar of the engine took
over.

Quickly Dad turned the key off, opened his door, and
jumped down to the ground. By the time I got out of
the truck Dad had the hood up and was holding one
hand out for me to stop.

"You don't want to see this," he said, sadly shaking his head.

But I wanted to see it. If I was really tough I had to look. I stood up on the bumper and peered down into the engine well. There was Miss Kitty II—my crazy cat-dog—chopped into pieces by the sharp fan blade. It was horrible.

By then Betsy was standing next to me. "Oh my God," she said. "It looks deli-sliced."

I didn't think it was so funny and suddenly my fake tough-guy pose vanished. It was horrible to see Miss Kitty II this way.

"I'm sorry," Dad said. He reached over and squeezed the back of my neck. "Sometimes cats sleep on top of engines because they are warm. This happens all the time."

I lowered my head and started to cry.

"Look out. Here we go again," Betsy sang. "The dike has let go. Everybody head for high ground before you drown."

"That's enough, Betsy," Dad said.

I turned and ran across our yard and into Tack's. I dove into the bushes by the side of their house and sobbed. If I hadn't tossed Miss Kitty II out my bedroom window she would have slept with me and not on the engine. "It's all my fault," I cried. I covered my eyes with my cupped hand. "I'm not tough at all." The tears dripped through the gaps in my fingers. I thought of water leaking up through the boards of a sinking boat.

After a few minutes I settled down and opened my eyes. I was facing one of Tack's narrow basement windows. I looked in. The ceiling light was on and I could see the pool table, the painted cross, and the words GONE BUT NOT FORGOTTEN. I hadn't forgotten. In an instant a fresh wave of tears streamed down my face. "Go ahead and cry," I said to myself. "It's okay. It's okay to cry at sad things. You have a whole lifetime to toughen up."

I hate to admit it, but Bitsy was right. I belonged in the Ripley Believe It Or Not Odditorium along with all the other freakish things. Any day now I expect the Ripley freak finders to pull up to our house and offer to buy me and

Adults Only

We were eating German noodles for dinner. Mom had served them covered with melted butter. I put one end in my mouth and sucked as hard as I could and watched with my eyes bugged out as the rest of the slippery noodle snaked through the maze on my plate. Slowly the entire mound of noodles began to spin around as they unraveled. Suddenly I remembered something incredible I had read in one of Jock Smith's bathroom magazines. It was about the history of food and the origins of the noodle. I bit off my noodle and as I chewed I blurted out, "I remember something!"

"Well forget it," Betsy replied.

"Kublai Khan made noodles popular among his soldiers by taking naked women, wrapping them with noodles and yak milk butter, and having them do a dinner striptease."

"What's a yak?" Pete asked.

"What comes out of his mouth," Betsy replied, pointing at me. "Yak, yak, yak."

"Where did you read that?" Mom asked me in a voice an octave higher than usual.

"At Tack Smith's house," I said. "His brother reads a lot of grown-up magazines."

"You mean *porno*?" Betsy asked, just trying to get me into trouble.

"What's porno?" Pete asked.

"Porno," Mom said firmly, "is not appropriate reading."

"Porno," Dad said, "is for adults only."

"It's not porno," I whined. "His magazines are about things men do, like fishing and race-car driving, and smoking cigars and making martinis." I could see Mom was still not pleased.

"I'm going to speak with his parents," she said, frowning. "I don't approve of that sort of magazine."

"Mom," I begged, "don't. They'll think I'm a big wuss."

"Then promise not to read them," she said.

I took a deep breath. "Okay," I said. "Promise, but I'm just trying to learn how to be a man."

"You can learn that around the house," Mom said. "Real men wash the dinner dishes."

"Then can I have some coffee to help me wake up?" I asked. "I'm beat. All day Mrs. Pierre had us practicing French folk dances for the spring talent show."

"No," Dad replied. "Coffee is for adults only."

"Betsy drinks it," I protested.

"As I said," Dad repeated. "It's for adults."

Betsy smirked and raised the cup to her lips. "Umm," she said. "This is so good. And I'm only having one little cup because I have self-control."

"Who cares?" I said, and got up from my seat and marched down the hall. But I did care. "Adults only," I muttered to Miss Kitty III. Tack's grandmother had sent her over the same day I buried Miss Kitty II. She was a typical gray-and-white cat. She slept a lot, purred when petted, scared a few mice, and explored all the nooks and crannies in the house. There wasn't a thing wrong with her, and yet I felt sorry for her already. I just had an odd feeling she wouldn't last long, and I turned out to be right.

After I washed the dishes I complained so much about being an abused kid Mom sent me to my room. "Go mope in private," she ordered. "Your constant whining is driving us nuts."

"Fine," I shot back. "Fine. I'll do just that. But keep in mind that my room is for Jack and Miss Kitty III *only*."

"Don't use that tone of voice on me, young man,"

Mom shot right back, and pointed toward the hall. "Now go."

I went into my room, opened my diary, and wrote, "Adults have the world rigged. They own everything. They get to do everything. And if kids complain, we are told to go to our rooms and mope in private. I don't like it one bit."

Just then Tack knocked on my window and poked his head in. "I've been waiting for your light to come on," he said. "I have another issue of *Argosy*."

"I'm not allowed to read that anymore," I said.

"Why?" he asked.

"I promised Mom I wouldn't read about man stuff."

"What she doesn't know won't hurt her," he said.

"True," I replied. "But I'm trying to be very adult and stick to my word."

"Why are you trying to be adult?" Tack asked.

"Because I want to do what they do, have what they have, go where they go."

"You're nuts," Tack said. "Adults are whacked. I never see them smile. All they do is work and worry. Really. Look at it this way, what do you love more, a puppy or a full-grown dog? Puppies rule," he said, answering his own question. "And we are the puppies of the world."

I wasn't going for it. "No way," I said. "Adults rule and we kiss their feet."

"You got it all backward," he said. "Adults work for us."

I rolled my eyes.

"Really," he said. "Adults have jobs, they have to pay the rent, buy cars, feed and clothe us, and what do we do? Hang out. Go to school. Goof off."

"Bunk," I said. "You forget their biggest job—telling us what to do!"

"You have a bad attitude," he said. "A chip on your shoulder. Leave the adults alone."

"No way," I whined. "Adults have a secret world of fun."

Tack laughed. "You've lost it, buddy. The last thing adults have is *fun*. Take a look at this." He held up the magazine. THE PRESIDENT'S SECRET LOVE NEST was splashed across the cover in black and red lettering. He flipped the magazine open and showed me the photos. The article was about the President's back-yard birdhouse. "Nothing in here would upset your mom," he concluded.

"Adults," I groaned. "They even trick each other with phony stories like this."

"Relax," Tack said. "Get over complaining about adults and enjoy your life."

"I'll try," I moaned, doubting my own efforts.

"Gotta go," he said. "Better get this back to Jock's bathroom before he finds it missing."

But I couldn't get over it. ADULTS ONLY signs were everywhere. In grocery stores there was a magazine section called ADULTS ONLY. Cigarette machines had signs announcing ADULTS ONLY. Clubs on Miami Beach had big signs flashing on and off, ADULTS ONLY. Liquor stores sold to ADULTS ONLY. School had private bathrooms for ADULTS ONLY.

One day we were driving past the Pleasure Island drive-in theater. It was ADULTS ONLY and sheltered behind a fence of tall Italian pines. I could see tiny swatches of jiggling pink flesh between the trees. I stared even harder. What was I seeing? Was it just the close-up of a nose? Or was it something I wasn't supposed to see because I was a kid?

Then I was in luck. At the far corner of the drive-in was a traffic light and it was red. As Dad braked, the bits of flesh between the trees slowed down and began to form into a solid image. It was a leg and . . . Suddenly Mom's hand was across my face.

"No looking," she said hastily. "That is strictly for adults."

"Have you ever been to a movie like that?" I asked.

"No," Dad said. "We're adults with kids. We don't have time to do adults-only stuff. Besides, I prefer movies where people keep their clothes on."

"I like keeping my clothes on," I said. "I don't like undressing in front of other people. I heard that in junior high you have to undress for gym class."

"It's no big deal," said Betsy. "It's just gym class. It's wholesome. It's not some striptease joint."

While she was talking my eyes wandered back to the screen. I couldn't believe what I was seeing.

"I told you, don't look," Mom scolded me. "Practice some self-control for a change. Self-control is what separates insects from animals, and animals from humans, and children from adults. Take some responsibility for your behavior. If you are so eager to be an adult all you have to do is act like one."

"I'm responsible," I said, defending myself.

"Only when someone is keeping an eye on you," said Betsy.

"I think those men's magazines have something to do with his new *interests*," Mom said to Dad. "I'm definitely going to speak with Tack's mother. Or his other mother, or whoever is in charge over there."

"We'll talk about this later," Dad said to her in a tone which meant the adults needed privacy to discuss my fate.

The next day after school, I went to the library.

"I need a book on becoming an adult," I said to Mrs. Marquette, the librarian.

"You mean, like on growing up?" she asked. "Becoming more mature, as in puberty?"

"Yeah," I said, not knowing exactly what she meant.

"Do you know that the most requested book in the library has never been checked out?" she said.

"What is it?" I asked.

"The book on becoming an adult," she replied.

"I heard about that book," I said. "Doesn't it have pictures?"

"Exactly," said the librarian. "All the kids ask for it, but they won't check it out."

"Why?" I asked.

"They need their parents' permission. Just as you will. I'll give you the form. Have your mom or dad sign it and come down here and pick it up." She opened a file cabinet and pulled out a permission sheet.

I took it to be polite. "Don't you have anything on becoming an adult that is not dangerous?" I asked.

"Nope," she said. "This is the only title the school board approved of."

"Are there any kids on the school board?" I asked, knowing the answer in advance.

She smiled. "Sorry," she said. "Adults only."

As soon as I left the library I balled up the permission slip and put it in the trash. I knew my parents were not going to okay a puberty book with body parts pictured in it.

I had some allowance money in my pocket so I decided to walk down to the strip mall. There was a bookstore and I thought, What could be more *adult* than taking personal responsibility and buying my own book on the subject rather than begging an adult to help me?

They had a lot of books on being a baby, but none on becoming an adult. But they did have a stack of old *Argosy* magazines. I checked over my shoulder to see if anyone was looking. The kid at the cash register was reading a comic book. I knew I was breaking a promise, so I quickly leafed through a copy to make sure there were no naked pictures. There were none. No harm done, I thought, and bought the magazine.

On my way home I went to the 7-Eleven to buy a bag of gummy worms. It was candy below my age level but I ate it anyway. It was kind of like still reading picture books even though I could read novels. But I didn't care. Picture books were fun, and gummy worms were good. I was standing in line when the person right behind me passed some paralyzing gas. It was silent, so I didn't hear it coming, but I could smell it when it arrived. It was deadly—cheesy and moist—and I pulled the neck of my T-shirt up over my mouth and breathed as if I was wearing a gas mask. I turned to glare at the person behind me. I expected to see some nasty wino, or Pepe LePew. Instead, it was an old lady with a sweet, pink face and twinkling eyes. She looked like a nun. When she smiled at me I turned away.

"That will be ninety-nine cents," the cashier said to me, then suddenly jerked her head back and wrinkled up her nose. "You should practice some self-control," she said.

I blushed, then looked again at the old lady. She raised her eyebrow, then held a delicate lace hankie up over her nose. "Young man, Bromo-Seltzer works for me," she said.

I spun back to the cashier. By now my face was on fire. "It's her," I whispered, and nodded toward the old woman who was holding a can of air freshener.

"Don't be rude," the cashier said, and propped her hands on her hips. "Just lay off the dairy products for a while."

I left as fast as I could. Adults, I thought to myself, get to blame everything on kids. And the older they are the more they get away with it. When I got home I hid my magazine under the mattress and went down to Betsy's room.

"Don't you think it is a raw deal?" I said to her. "Adults get everything."

"That's why they are adults," she said as she sewed loose buttons on a blouse. "They can handle it. You can't."

"What do you mean?" I said.

"I mean that you don't have the self-control to make decisions and manage your life the way an adult does," she said.

"Not true," I replied.

"It is too true," she said. "You have no idea how to manage your behavior."

"Not so," I protested.

"Okay," she said. "Don't take my word for it. I'll give you a test. Tomorrow, when we all go over to the Guggies for dinner, I want you to fake sick and stay home by yourself. The true definition of a person's character and maturity is what kind of behavior they have when no one is looking."

"What do you mean?" I asked.

"I mean," she said, "right now you have two kinds of behavior. There is the sneaky Jack, like when you drink out of the milk carton while standing in front of the refrigerator when no one is looking. But if Mom is around you pour the milk in a glass like the good boy Jack. Your *true* self is the one that drinks out of the carton. The *fake* self is the one that only does stuff because otherwise you'd be in trouble. In other words, you have no self-control. No inner strength. So you shouldn't be allowed to do what adults do."

"You must think I'm some sort of caveman," I said. "I have self-control."

"Fine," she said. "You don't have to prove it to me. You just have to prove it to yourself. Tomorrow put yourself to the test and find out if you have inner strength or if you need to be constantly watched over like a baby in order to do the right things in life."

"Okay," I said defiantly. "I'll do it."

The next day when everyone else got ready to go to the Guggies I went up to Mom. "I don't feel well," I said, and put a fake sick look on my face.

"Pull yourself together," Mom replied, as she flicked her feathered hair into place.

"I'd rather stay home and rest in bed," I said.

"You'll be fine," she said, not paying much attention to me.

"I think I'm going to barf," I yelped, and ran down the hall. I lifted the toilet seat and made a series of beastly belching noises. Then I filled my mouth up with water from the sink and spurted it into the toilet bowl. "Arggghh," I groaned.

I wiped my mouth on my sleeve and returned to Mom.

"That didn't sound very good," she said.

"I'm just going to get into bed and take it easy," I said. "I think it is the *adult* thing to do. The *childish* thing to do would be to come with you then barf all over the dinner table."

"I think you're right," she agreed. "Now go put on your pj's. Miss Kitty III can keep you company."

I did, then got into bed. Mom gave me the Guggies' phone number just in case I began to die. "And no funny business," she warned me.

"Don't treat me like a child," I whined.

"Don't let Tack bring those magazines over here," she said, getting to the point.

"Mom, I won't read his magazines," I said, knowing that I had my own.

"Fine," she said, and walked off.

Betsy stuck her head in my door. "Remember," she sang. "What you do when no one is looking is the real you."

"I get it," I said. "Just leave."

As soon as they were gone I hopped out of bed. The only sounds made were mine. Somehow they scared me because they were supposed to say so much about me. The floor creaked when I walked across it. What could that mean? The curtains flapped like huge bird wings in the breeze. And when I flushed the toilet the noise seemed as loud as the sinking of the Titanic.

I sat down on a chair in the living room. Do not turn on the TV, I said to myself. Not the radio either. Just sit and think, like an adult. These were my rules. Betsy told me that it took a lot of courage to really want to know who I was, and if I was adult enough, I just needed to sit quietly and listen to my own thoughts.

My nose itched. I picked it. Then I stopped picking it. Betsy had said if I were an adult I would not pick my nose. She said if I was still a kid I would pull out a big nose-nugget then squeeze it between my thumb and finger and roll it into a ball and flick it across the room or stick it under the seat of a chair. I had done that before. And worse. I had cleaned food out of my teeth with a pencil point, spit loogies into the kitchen sink, picked the underwear lint out of the crack in my butt, jammed my little finger halfway into my ear to dig out some wax which I then sniffed, and hollered curse words when I stubbed my toe on a chair. I peed all over the toilet seat and didn't wipe it clean, scraped the toe jam out from under my nails with a dinner knife that I put back in the drawer without washing it. But that was all in the past. Now I was a mature adult. And mature adults didn't do any of that stuff anymore. They had conquered childish behavior.

So I sat in the chair in the living room with my hands on my lap and my feet flat on the floor. I had on a clean pair of pj's. I had on clean socks. I had good posture and a smile on my face.

"This," I said out loud to Miss Kitty III as she slept on the couch, "is the real me."

Almost immediately the echo of a voice in the back of my head said, "No, this is not the real you. Don't lie to yourself. The real you is the other you, the one who drinks out of the milk carton." After about thirty seconds I couldn't stand sitting still anymore. I thought my head would explode from all the quiet. "You know what you really want to do," I said to myself. "Now go do it! Be the real Jack."

I hopped up out of my chair, jumped over the couch, and got busy.

We did not have air-conditioning and it was already hot. So first, I created my own total comfort zone. I opened the refrigerator door and pulled a chair up to hold it open. I put the portable television from Mom's room on another chair. I skipped down to my bedroom and got my magazine and my gummy worms. Then I took my refrigerated seat, tuned in the baseball game, and propped my feet up on an inside shelf. "Now this is living," I said, and reached for a pot of cold German noodles. Miss Kitty III joined me. There was a plate of leftover meat loaf on a low shelf. I pulled off the plastic wrap and she picked at that while I moved on and worked over an old piece of fried chicken. After I chewed off all the good stuff, I tossed the bones and skin into the refrigerator so Miss Kitty III could finish the rest.

I started to read an article in the magazine on how successful men properly trim nose hair, but after a paragraph I was bored. I flipped through the other articles. It was all pretty dull. "You've been to the Elks Club with Dad enough to know how a grown man should behave," I said to myself. I put the magazine down next to a bowl of cucumber salad and took out the Cheez Whiz. I opened the top and dipped a gummy worm in. As I ate it I thought to myself, This is the real me and there is not a thing wrong with it. I'm just misunderstood by adults. Any kid my age would agree that at this moment I was living the good life. I popped open a soda and drank almost all of it down. I could feel a huge burp growing inside my belly like a nuclear mushroom cloud waiting to let loose. I held it in and glanced up at the clock. As soon as the second hand was over the twelve I let it loose. I sounded like a yodeling bullfrog and when I finished I looked up at the clock and smiled. "That glorious sound," I said to Miss Kitty III, "was eight seconds of pure belching pleasure."

Then I really let myself go. I picked my nose some more, wiped my mouth on my sleeve, opened the back door and spit out any food I didn't like, sang way out of tune, and swore at the TV anytime the other team did something good.

This was living. This was the real me.

Suddenly, headlights swept past the window and Dad's car turned up the driveway. "Emergency!" I shouted. "Go, go, go." I hopped up and jumped into action. I slammed the refrigerator door shut, pushed the chairs back to the dining-room table, and carried Mom's TV back up to her room. I got it plugged in just as they opened the front door. In an instant I sprinted to my room and slipped into bed. Safe.

Betsy was the first one to check up on me. "Well," she said. "How did it go?"

"Piece of cake," I said, adjusting my pillow and giving a fake yawn. "I sat in the living room, read a book, and listened to opera on the radio. Finally, I got tired, washed my face, flossed and brushed my teeth, said my prayers, and went directly to sleep. Totally adult behavior."

"Very impressive," Betsy replied. Still, I could tell by the tone of her voice she was suspicious. But she could never prove a thing.

Mom was next. "How are you feeling, sweetie?" she asked, and pressed her palm against my forehead.

"Fine," I said. "Better."

"Was Miss Kitty III good company?" she asked, and lifted her hand.

"The best," I said. "She's a very mature cat."

After Mom left I turned off my light and lay in bed looking up at the ceiling. I guess I am a combination of two types of people, I thought. I have a secret life as a guy doing guy stuff, and when I'm in public I live a perfect life of manners and refinement. And there will be no witnesses to judge the difference. No harm done, I thought.

I was the first one up as usual. Our school was overcrowded with all the kids like me whose families had moved down to Florida for the construction boom. There were a lot of new jobs building houses and businesses, but they still hadn't built enough new schools. So we were on a split shift at South Miami Elementary. The fourth, fifth, and sixth graders were on the early shift and so every morning when I woke up it was still dark.

I quietly walked down the hall and went into the kitchen. I whipped open the refrigerator door and was reaching for the orange juice when I saw her—Miss Kitty III. She was stiff from the cold. I put my hand over my mouth and stopped myself from screaming as I closed the door. "Oh my," I said, talking out loud like a crazy person, "how did this happen?"

Then I said, "This is a joke. Pete or Betsy tricked me and I bet it's a stuffed animal they made up to look like

Miss Kitty III." Slowly, I opened the refrigerator door again and peeked inside. It didn't look like a toy stuffed animal. It looked more like one of my Uncle Jim's stuffed foxes. But there was no doubt about it, it *was* Miss Kitty III. Her gray paw was still raised up in the air with her claws sticking out where she'd been furiously scratching the inside of the door. "Oh God, not this again," I cried out in despair. I stepped back, closed the door and asked myself, *How could this happen?* It was obvious that the cat did not open the door herself. Someone must have come into the kitchen in the middle of the night to get water. They opened the refrigerator door in order to get some light. Then they turned around and opened the cupboard and reached for a glass. At that moment the cat must have seen the open refrigerator door and climbed in to explore. Then whoever the person was must have turned back around, poured cold water out of the pitcher into their glass, then quickly closed the door and returned to bed. This left Miss Kitty III trapped inside while her muffled cries went unheard. But who did it?

I opened the door again to make sure this wasn't all a nightmare. "Oh," I said when I got a good look at all the desperate scratch marks on the inside of the door.

Just then I heard Pete start down the hall. He liked to get up after me so I could make him toast with butter and jam. I thought, Should I tell him about Miss Kitty III? *No,* I decided. There was only one way to catch the culprit. I had to surprise him. I stood to the side of the refrigerator where I could get a good look at Pete's face to see if it showed signs of guilt.

"Good morning," he said sleepily.

"Top o' the day to you," I replied, just as he opened the door. In about two seconds he started to let out a horror movie scream but I leapt forward and covered his mouth.

"Settle down," I said, and removed my hand. "It's too late to do anything about it now." Then I heard Betsy come down the hall. "Hush," I whispered to Pete. "This'll be good."

When she came around the corner Pete and I were standing next to the refrigerator looking totally innocent.

Betsy smirked at us. "What are you two morons up to this morning?" she asked.

"Just being morons," I replied as she opened the refrigerator door.

"Oh my God!" she shouted and slammed it. She glared at me. "Is this your sick idea of a joke?" she snapped.

"Relax," I said. "We don't know how it happened. Now stand over here with us," I said. "Mom's coming."

When Mom turned the corner she was yawning and rubbing her eyes. "How come the three of you are so quiet and not fighting yet this morning?" she asked.

"We called a truce," I replied. "You know, like in the old wars when both sides would call a cease-fire so they could remove the dead bodies from the battlefield."

"Charming," Mom muttered, then asked, "Have you seen Miss Kitty III?"

"Nope," I replied.

"Not yet," Betsy said.

Pete twisted his head, no.

Then Mom opened the refrigerator door. She reached in for the coffee cream and didn't seem to notice anything weird. She's not wearing her glasses, I thought. But then she stooped down to reach for the cream cheese and pretty much shook Miss Kitty III's hand. Her mouth opened but no sound came out. I leapt forward and grabbed her before she let loose a bloodcurdling scream.

"It's okay," I said to her. "Well, maybe not okay, but there is nothing we can do about it."

"How did it happen?" she asked.

"I'm trying to figure that out," I said.

I could hear Dad coming down the hall and by the time he turned the corner we were standing in a huddle next to the refrigerator.

"What are you all up to this morning?" he asked.

"Just having a loving family moment," Mom replied, and gave him a crooked smile.

He opened the door, paused, then slowly turned and looked at us. "Good Lord," he said. "Who killed this one?"

"Not me," said Pete.

"Certainly wasn't me," Betsy said emphatically.

"Innocent," Mom said.

Then everyone looked at me. "I didn't have anything to do with it!" I cried out.

"But who else could it be?" said Betsy, bearing down and poking me in the chest with her finger. "You are the only cat serial killer in this house. Now confess!"

"Yes!" everyone said at once. "Confess!"

Without a doubt in their minds they had me pegged as the killer of Miss Kitty III. But it wasn't me this time. They were just judging me by my reputation.

"I can prove I'm innocent," I shouted, and thumped myself on the chest with my fist.

"Then prove it," Betsy said arrogantly. "Go right ahead. We are all waiting to hear your explanation."

I knew what I had to do. I ran up the hall and into Pete's room. There was no water glass next to his bed. I ran into Mom and Dad's room. No water glass. I checked the bathroom. No glass. Then I ran into Betsy's room. The water glass was right on her bedside table next to her allergy medicine. I smiled a very big smile to myself as I held the glass behind my back and marched into the kitchen.

I looked Betsy directly in the eye. "How come you

aren't sneezing this morning?" I asked, sounding as genuinely concerned about her health as possible.

She looked at me suspiciously.

"Answer him," Dad ordered. He had taken over as judge on the case.

"Because I took my medicine last night," she replied. "*Before* I went to the Guggies." She took the glass from my hand and sniffed it. "Iced coffee," she said. "Two days old."

"I don't believe you," I said.

"Just hold your horses, Sherlock," she replied. "We all ate at the Guggies and when we came home we went to bed. There was only one person at home with the cat last night. You! And it's my guess that you were eating like a pig in front of the refrigerator again and the cat got inside. Then the car pulled up in the driveway, you panicked because you were supposed to be in bed, so you slammed the door and Miss Kitty was still inside."

"Impossible," I said. "I was in bed the whole time. I didn't do it. It couldn't have been me." Yet, as I defended myself, a cold feeling went up my spine. As cold as Miss Kitty III. It had to be me. And I knew Betsy was right. I just didn't have the inner strength to confess. I couldn't say, Yes, it was my fault, like an adult would.

"Well, *whoever* is responsible for this," Dad said, "knows it in their heart. And I for one, sure wouldn't want to live with myself."

Again, I wanted to blurt out, It was me! But I didn't

have the guts to say so. Instead, I looked Betsy in the eye and asked, "Where is your evidence?"

"Well," she replied, "it just so happens that while you were collecting dirty glasses I did a bit of snooping on my own." She held out the jar of Cheez Whiz with the gummy worm still in it. In her other hand she had the chicken bones. "Signs that Jack has been here," she said. "Plus look at the food fingerprints all over the refrigerator door."

"That could be anyone," I said desperately.

"But I have more evidence," she said coldly, staring directly into my eyes.

Suddenly it struck me. Where was the magazine? Mom would kill me if she knew I broke a promise.

"An adult would own up to their actions," Betsy said, giving me another chance to do the adult thing.

I was mute. I didn't know what would be worse. Owning up to killing Miss Kitty, or having Betsy show Mom the magazine.

"A responsible, secure person would admit their mistake and learn from it," Betsy said, applying pressure.

I couldn't take it anymore. "It was me," I said meekly, with my head bowed. "It was an accident."

Mom just stared at me with tears in her eyes, and shook her head. "Poor Miss Kitty," she cried.

"I'm telling Tack," Pete hollered.

"I don't know what has gotten into you," Dad said.

"I'm just trying to be an adult," I explained.

"Well, I have news for you," he replied. "Whatever you're doing, it's not working."

No one had anything more to say to me. "I'll take care of Miss Kitty III from here," I said. "I've had some experience with this sort of thing."

As soon as everyone left I put a plastic bag over Miss Kitty III and took her out the back door. I walked down to the shed and got the shovel. And then I did what I had already done two times before. Only this time I wished I could crawl into the hole with Miss Kitty III and shovel the dirt back up over myself. As I dug I looked at my cat. "When you have no self-control," I said to her, and myself, "there is no such thing as *no harm done*."

When I returned to my room Betsy was waiting for me.

"You left this in the kitchen," she said, and handed me the magazine.

"Well, I won't be needing that anymore," I said. "I plan to remain a kid for as long as I can."

"You don't have a choice," Betsy said.

She was right. I was a kid and there was no reason to fight it. "So, why'd you let me off the hook?" I asked.

"Because the only way to become an adult is for *you* to make the right choices," she said. "And confessing was a good start."

"One more thing," I said. "What do you do when you're home alone?"

"Believe it or not!" she snapped. "Sometimes I'm just thinking about how to help you grow up and keep you from becoming a pathetic-boy display in the Ripley's Odditorium!" Then she turned, walked down to the kitchen, and made herself a cup of coffee.

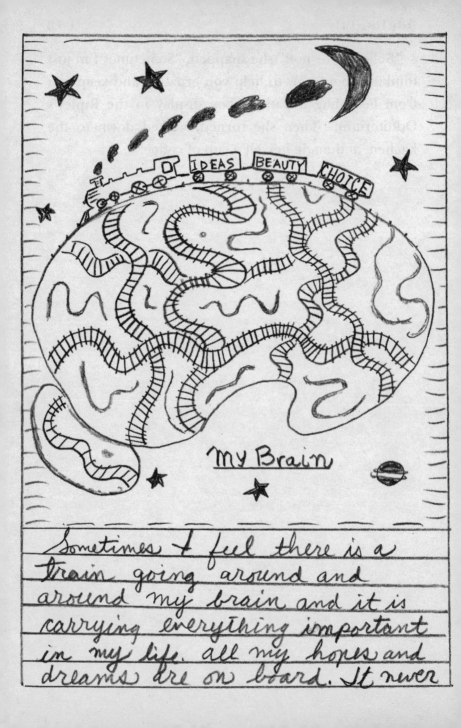

My Brain

Sometimes I feel there is a train going around and around my brain and it is carrying everything important in my life. all my hopes and dreams are on board. It never

Beauty and Order

Summer was almost here. It was already hot in the early morning and I was sitting out back staring beyond our yard toward the dandelions and train tracks. All day, every day, the long freight trains rumbled back and forth. They brought in lumber, cement, steel beams, roof tiles, nails, tools, bulldozers, earthmovers, fishing boats, cars, and people. South Florida was being built up with things made in places that had already been built up. We wanted what they had, and they wanted what we had. On the return trip the trains carried huge royal palm trees, pallets of coral block and limestone cut right from the earth, and crates of oranges, limes, and grapefruit. It was as if all of South Florida was being replaced. The trees, swamps, alligators, flamingos, Seminole Indians, and fish were being taken away. Before long we'd be filled up with pieces of Ohio, New Jersey, Indiana, and Michigan. Soon, those states would look like ours. But I wondered if such enormous changes really would work. I didn't think you could just mix everything up. Some things would change for the worse if moved. When icebergs broke away from the Arctic, I reminded myself, they melted down to nothing on their way south.

Just as Florida was building on the outside, I was building on the inside, where no one could see the changes taking place. Even I couldn't see them. Still, I knew trainloads of ideas made up in my brain and feelings leaping out of my heart were shifting around within me. It was confusing to try and figure out what was going on. Sometimes it felt as if my brain was growing faster than my skull and my head would explode. All I knew was that I woke with some pressure building up inside me where I didn't yet have the words to express it. Whatever change was going to take place was still a mystery to me. Caterpillars must have felt the same way before they dozed off to burst awake later as butterflies.

The thought of all this oncoming change made me nervous, so I rolled my sleeve up and checked on my hookworm. Now, that was something I could see. I didn't know how I got it. Three days before, it just appeared. The first day the worm had made a little mark, the size of a comma, on my forearm. Once I knew he was busy I kept monitoring his progress. He was a hard-working worm. He never slept. Even in the middle of the night he was still at it.

At the end of the second day the spiral had circled around twice and he was picking up speed. By the third day I looked as if I had pressed my forearm down over an electric-stove burner. But I still wasn't ready to get rid of him. He was a secret pet and, unlike me, he would never change. On and on forever, like every other hookworm on the planet, he would spiral around. He didn't make straight lines or zigzags or figure eights. Only spirals. I wished my life was as simple as his. But I knew better. Life had more in store for me than just going in circles.

My only fear was that he'd finish his job on my arm when I wasn't watching and move to a fresh place like the inside of my eye, where he'd spiral around and around, and drill it through before moving on to do the same with my brain. Sooner or later I'd have to get some medicine, but not yet. I rolled my sleeve back down and went inside.

"Is my ride here yet?" I asked Mom. We were almost finished with the school year. Mrs. Pierre was sick of us and we were sick of her. It was only a matter of moments before the entire class went insane and everyone was at each other's throats. All year long there wasn't money for anything special, then suddenly we were taken on a field trip almost every week. We had been to the Planetarium, the Seaquarium, the Parrot Jungle, and the Monkey Jungle. Now we were going to Vizcaya, a huge old mansion filled with French art and furniture. It was now a museum.

"No," Mom said. She was gluing on a new set of red fingernails and waiting for her ride to work. The glue smelled like burning plastic and made the inside of my nose sting.

Suddenly there was a knock on the door. We both stood up and stepped forward. I turned the doorknob because Mom's nails weren't dry yet.

It was Tack, and he was holding up a fluffy white cat. It looked as if it had been groomed for a cat show, with its fur combed and puffed out like cotton candy around a tiny pink face. "I told my grandmother what happened," he said. "She was very sorry and wants you to have this special cat."

"I'm sorry too," I whispered, and lowered my chin. I was still upset about Miss Kitty III.

"She said the refrigerator disaster had happened to her before," he said. "She wanted me to make sure and tell you that."

"Thanks," I replied.

"It's just like the cat on the car engine, or on the tracks," he said. "It happens to other people too."

"I'm sure it does," I said, "but it doesn't make it any better. I'm the kiss of death for these cats." I reached out and took it from his arms.

"Well, don't kiss them anymore," he said, then laughed through his nose with such force a long strand of thick yellow snot unrolled from his nostril like a party whistle, then snapped back.

"Don't you think she's beautiful?" Tack asked.

It was a beautiful cat but I didn't care if it looked like Miss America. I was staring at Tack's nostril. The way the snot had unrolled into a long strand then rolled back up into his nose was pretty incredible to me. Lately I was beginning to wonder why I was much more interested in gross things than beautiful things. This was starting to bother me about myself. I found it puzzling and I was worried it would become a problem.

"What are you going to name it?" Tack asked.

"Miss Kitty IV," Mom replied.

"Don't you think we should break the cycle?" I suggested. "Give it a name, like Supercat, or Mightycat, or something tough like Spike?"

"Yes," she said. "How about Wonder Woman?"

Just then a van pulled up and a kid inside waved to me.

"See you later," I said to Mom, and handed her Wonder Woman. She frowned as its fur stuck to her nails.

"Have fun," Tack groaned. He was at a different school and they were doing nothing but math drills.

I took a seat in the back of the van next to a girl I hadn't talked with all year long because she was on the other side of Mrs. Pierre's gender wall. There was a big burn mark on the lap of her dress. It was the first thing

I spotted because it smelled like burnt toast. She caught me staring and tried to cover it with her hands. I didn't know what to say to her so I pointed at the blackened circle and asked, "Did you set yourself on fire?"

She turned toward me. She had outrageously thick glasses. Behind them, her eyeballs looked like huge blue guppies trapped inside very tiny fish tanks.

"It was an accident," she said. "As I waited for the van I was sitting and reading a book on the sidewalk. The sun was behind me and felt good on my back. And I was so involved in the story that I didn't notice the sun shining through a corner of my glasses like a magnifying glass and focusing a hot spot of light on my dress and so it caught fire."

"Wow," I remarked, thinking to myself that she was so honest. If I had stupidly set myself on fire I never would have told anyone.

"Have you ever done anything stupid?" she asked.

I had done a million stupid things but I was too embarrassed to say so. "No," I replied. I tried to look her in the eyes but because I was lying I stared down at my shoes.

"Have you ever been to Vizcaya before?" she asked.

"No," I said. "Never even heard of it."

"It's my favorite place in Miami," she said. "It's beautiful."

Hope you don't stare at it for too long then, I thought, or you'll burn it down.

———

When we arrived at Vizcaya, Mrs. Pierre lined us up in two rows, one for girls and one for boys.

"The girls will appreciate the mansion," she announced. "But house *décor* won't be of much interest to you boys. If you wish, you can run off and play in the gardens." She pointed toward the distant acres of hedges and canals. "There are plenty of snakes and snails out there."

A boy named Wilson, who had never shown interest in his schoolwork, said, "You mean we can just run around?"

"Like wild Indians," Mrs. Pierre suggested, and threw one hand up over her head as if she held a tomahawk, while her other hand patted her lips. "Woo, woo, woo," she whooped.

I hated how Mrs. Pierre, and other people too, thought they understood what I liked or disliked just because I was a boy. Some people were as well trained as hookworms and never grew beyond the custom that blue is for boys and pink is for girls. I guessed it was a lot easier to be lazy and stupid and just lump all the boys together, rather than have to sort through them and find out what each one liked and disliked. I decided to stay with the girls while the boys took off.

Just then a very old man rounded the corner and stood in front of us. He was dressed in a suit jacket that probably fit him when he was young and not stooped over. His tie was frayed, and immediately I noticed that he must have had a hair transplant because his scalp was lined with rows of evenly spaced plugs of hair like a miniature cornfield.

"Hello," he wheezed, and smiled so broadly that his wrinkled cheeks unfolded like an accordion. "My name is Mr. Adolino and I am your guide at Vizcaya. Please follow me."

We all poked forward behind him. As we entered the front door someone stepped on the back of my shoe and my foot popped out. I turned around to see who did it but no one confessed. I stepped and scuffed, stepped and scuffed forward like a man with one bum leg. To one side of the foyer was a door marked with a telephone sign. I slipped inside. It was a plain, sea-green room with a comfortable old leather chair next to a telephone. I sat down and untied my shoe, and refit my foot. When I looked up I was surprised to see a bouquet of enormous roses painted on the ceiling. They were the most milky wet, red, and creamy gold roses I had ever seen. As I stared up at them my heart began to race and I felt nervous. At first I thought my nervousness was because the beauty was as strong and blinding as looking into the sun. Then, just as I felt I would faint, I jerked my head away and closed my eyes. I took a deep breath, then looked back at the roses, and once again, just when I thought I would reach into the painting and hold them in my hands and be swallowed up by the velvet petals, I jerked my eyes away and looked down at the floor, where somebody had spit out a piece

of gum. It was black with dirt and in some sick spasm of
a thought I imagined having to scrape up the gum and
chew it, and I was revolted with the thought of it.

Why am I turning away from beauty, I asked myself,
only to stare at gross, filthy, disgusting things? I didn't
have the answer. And by the time I fled the telephone
room everyone had gone. I thought I heard Mr. Adolino's voice explaining something about the "classical
Adams wall treatments," so I went the other way. I
wanted to test a theory I was developing about myself.
With Tack, I had looked at his nasty snot before looking
at the beautiful cat. And with the girl I had been more
interested in her burned dress and weird eyes than her
honesty. Since I was in such a beautiful mansion I
wanted to see if I could just enjoy beauty and not be so
totally captivated with gross stuff.

I passed down a long hallway and entered a fancy
music room. A sign mounted in a small brass frame de-
scribed the room as "Austrian Baroque." From a small
overhead speaker classical violin music was playing. I
closed my eyes and the music formed the image of large
fern buds curling open in slow motion. I opened my
eyes before someone sneaked up on me. In one corner
of the room was a harpsichord and a beautiful, hand-
painted harp of polished blond wood. I looked at the
top of the harp and began to follow the bend of
the wood with my eye. The watery swirl of the music,
the image of curling ferns, and the curve of the harp all
braided together into something so beautiful to me I

suddenly jerked my head away and stared down at the baseboard where there was a narrow heating vent clogged with dust, bits of dirty paper, and insects. I felt as if I could have stared at the vent for hours. It was such a relief after the shock of so much beauty. Suddenly the music overhead sounded less like flowing violins and more like someone weeping. I closed my eyes again and tried to change what I was feeling, but the room had already given me the creeps and I marched out as if I knew where I was going.

But I didn't. I ended up in a room with a bronze statue of a Greek boy sitting on a tree stump pulling a thorn out of his foot. His face was set in an expression of absolute concentration. The bow-shaped wrinkles across his forehead were perfectly formed. His eyes squinted. And his lips were so tightly pressed together that I felt my lips pinch back against my teeth. I felt exactly what he felt. But instead of feeling the thorn in my foot, I pulled my eyes away and found myself rolling up my sleeve to check on my hookworm. My eyes went around the spiral again and again until I reached the outward tip. I pulled my pen out of my pocket and began to pick and scratch at the spot where the hookworm was digging. Finally I broke through my skin and gouged out a hunk of flesh, or worm. I didn't know which. I dropped it on the black marble floor and stepped on it. When I lifted my shoe there was a pasty pink spot of crushed something. I looked back at my forearm. A little line of blood had rolled down the side.

I wiped it off on my pants, then dashed out the door.

I climbed a set of stairs that led to a guest bedroom. The walls were covered with elaborate Chinese scenes of birds and cherry blossoms buzzing with glossy insects. The bed was draped with pink silk with gold fringe. I stepped back so I could take it all in when suddenly my eyes drifted toward the bottom edge of the bed covering, where there was a splash of a crimson stain. And once I saw the stain my eyes fixed on it and wouldn't let go until I blinked and quickly looked down at the floor. I stood there for a few minutes until the words gathered in my mind like a jury. And I knew what I suspected about myself was true. That I was more attracted to totally gross things than to beautiful things.

I returned down the stairwell and found the closest exit. I left the house as quickly as possible and began to walk aimlessly through the maze of low hedges. Suddenly I saw, lying in the middle of the path, a mauled squirrel. I stared into the open wound of his belly. The flesh was surrounded with a crowd of buzzing, shiny blue flies. I found myself staring at the flies, at the glistening flesh, and the stiff fur standing out on the rigid body. Why, I wondered, can I not concentrate on a work of art but can stare like an eagle at the slightest object of filth, death, and decay? This horrified me because it meant that Mrs. Pierre was right—that boys could only like snakes and snails and puppy dogs' tails and all things disgusting, gross, and weird. But I didn't want that to be true. I loved beautiful objects. It

couldn't be true, because it was a man who built and
furnished this house. Something had to be wrong with
me.

I was thinking about all of this when I passed through
a stone arch and entered a walled, secret garden. The
girl with the burned dress was sitting on a bench reading a book. She had been so honest in the car about her
burn mark that I thought I might try being totally honest too. I really didn't have anyone else to confide in.
Tack wouldn't understand and I hadn't made close
friends with any of the other boys in my class. "Hi," I
said. She looked up from her book.

"I'm sitting in the shade," she said, as her huge eyes
dipped down toward her dress. "No more fire acci-
dents."

"You asked if I ever did something stupid," I said.
"Well, I lied. I've been doing something really stupid all
day long. Every time I look at something beautiful I get
so nervous I have to look away at something disgusting
to settle down."

"What do you mean?" she asked.

"I mean, I'll look at a beautiful painting and it's as if
I've just stuck my finger over a flame. I can only keep
my eyes on the painting for about three seconds before
I jerk them away. And then, the worst part is I immediately find something gross and filthy to look at which I
find a kind of relief from all that beauty. Now, don't you
think something is wrong with that?"

She looked at me very carefully, and her large eyes passed over me as if she were looking for cracks in a glass. After a minute she said, "That's awful. My sister had a problem kind of like that," she said. "She couldn't find anything nice to say about people. She could only find nasty things to say. And you know what they say, 'If you can't say something nice, don't say anything at all.' Well, she didn't follow that rule, and it only got worse. Her mouth was going a mile a minute just saying mean things all day long."

"What happened next?" I asked. I was really interested because I was a lot like the sister too. I never had a nice thing to say to Betsy, I bullied Pete, and I seemed to spend a lot of time thinking about everyone's worst qualities.

"We put her in a hospital for a while. She's home now. And she's better, but she has to take medication to stay nice. Otherwise she gets mean again."

"Do you think my problem is like her problem?" I asked.

"It's not exactly the same," she said. "But I'd be really upset if looking at beautiful things made me feel so nervous that I had to look at ugly things in order to feel better."

"What do you think I should do?" I asked.

"My mom says that the only way to chart a course in life is to use all your strengths to defeat all your weaknesses."

I knew she was telling me something important. The more I realized this the less I listened to her. In fact, listening to her was the same as if I was looking at something beautiful or listening to wonderful music. After a few seconds of listening my eyes drifted from hers to the lily pond just to her side. In a windblown corner the dirty water had been whipped up into a bubbly brown foam of decaying leaves and twigs and insects. It looked like a hunk of rotting fat and seemed as if at any minute some horrible monster would spontaneously rise from out of the scum.

When I jerked my eyes back toward her she was staring at me. "Did you hear what I said?" she asked, a bit irritated.

"I have to go," I suddenly replied, embarrassed and looking away again. "I need to sit down and think for a while."

I turned and walked up a stone path lined with perfectly boxed hedges. I had never seen leaves so well trimmed and controlled. It seemed against their nature. I felt the same when I watched trained animals at the circus. I once saw a lion tamer stick his entire head inside a lion's mouth. I wasn't impressed by the bravery of the lion tamer. Instead, I was puzzled when the lion didn't snap his head off. It only seemed natural that he would.

The thought that leaves and wild animals had more control over themselves than I had over my own mind made me feel uncomfortable. Dad had told me a million times that a disciplined mind was the most important quality to have in life. He said any person with a chaotic mind was destined for a pitiful life of confusion and sadness. He was right. And I was the living proof.

Along the path were a series of classical statues on marble pedestals. Every now and again I glanced up at them then quickly looked down at my shoes, which were chalky with coral dust. One of the pedestals was vacant. A small plastic sign on it read, STATUE REMOVED FOR REPAIR. On impulse I lifted the sign and tossed it behind a hedge. Then I climbed up on top and struck a pose.

I didn't know exactly how to stand. I didn't know what to do with my hands. I didn't know where to look. To my left was a statue of an old man hunched over in agony. To my right was a woman draped in carved robes and carrying a large bowl in her hands. I remembered the statue *The Thinker* with his head leaning forward onto his fist, so I put my pointer finger against my temple, squinted, and tilted my head in thought. I imagined myself frozen in time with my mind focused on some lofty idea. But after a minute I figured I looked more like the dopey Scarecrow from *The Wizard of Oz* than a classical figure deep in thought. I can't even think nice thoughts about myself, I said. I felt so depressed I sat down on the pedestal with my chin dropped down against my chest.

When I looked up again I spotted two men pushing a small cart as they went about collecting trash from big green cans. That will be my job someday, I thought. It will be a perfect fit for me. I love looking at garbage so much I can make a career out of it.

I took a deep breath and began to think. If I had to make a choice about what kind of person I would be in life, I'd choose to admire what was beautiful and thoughtful and honest, not disgusting and ugly. So how did it happen that I fell into the bad habit of only looking at gross things, thinking mean thoughts, and not always telling the truth? How did I let such awful things happen to me without knowing? It was like there was a hookworm of ugliness gouging out all that was smart and good in my heart and mind.

Something was all mixed up inside me and I wanted it to be straightened out. I had seen that I was one way, when I wanted to be another. That's what this whole day was all about. It was pointing out that the beautiful things I wanted to love were on a collision course with the gross things I found so attractive. It was up to me to make the right decision about what I wanted, and have the strength to break away from the old, bad habits while getting new ones. I could steer myself away from what I didn't like and toward what I did like. It was possible.

I closed my eyes and sat as still as a statue. I didn't move a muscle, but inside me trainloads of screaming thoughts were crisscrossing from my fingertips to my toes. It felt as if the force of those speeding thoughts was just as powerful as the trains roaring through my back yard. And it seemed to me that just as I could be killed by standing in front of a speeding train, I could be killed by standing in the way of a powerful thought.

Now, it was as if two giant trains had raced toward me from different directions. One carried a cargo of beauty, kindness, and truth. The other held only ugliness. The conflict was forcing me to make a choice that would change my life for all the other days before me. But suddenly it was like those old movies where two trains collide, and when the dust settled something new inside me had been created.

I stood up on the pedestal and looked down the line of classical statues. Their noses were chipped. Some were missing arms. Fingers were snapped off. But it didn't matter. They were still beautiful and always would be. I closed my eyes again and lifted my chin. I stood there feeling the sun shine warmly across my face until the glow of it filled my mind with a golden light. I could have stood there forever.

In the distance, Mrs. Pierre called out, "Snakes and snails and puppy dogs' tails! Sugar and spice and everything nice! It's time to go home! *Allez, allez!*"

I saw the girl with the big eyes walking from the secret garden toward the driveway. She held a book with her finger between the pages as if a giant clam shell had snapped shut on her.

"Hey," I yelled out. "Wait up." As she turned toward me I jumped off the pedestal.

"What were you doing up there?" she asked.

At first I thought it was too embarrassing to tell her what I had been thinking. But then I did. I told her about how my whole day had built up into one important turning point in my life.

"Wow," she said. "I hope I get a day like that."

"I don't think you want a lot of them," I replied. "Just enough to keep you on track."

"The only thing I learned today was to read in the shade," she said.

"It all adds up," I replied. "You'll see. It all comes together at once and you have to have the guts to do something about it."

When we reached the driveway kids were showing up from all directions. "Clap, clap," Mrs. Pierre called out and clapped her hands as if they were cymbals. "The ball is over. Time to go home and become pumpkins again."

We climbed back into our van and began to edge down the long driveway. I turned and stared at the mansion. It was magnificent. I thought of my house. It tilted to the side just a bit. It was missing shingles. The shutters sagged. I smiled just thinking about it because now it reminded me of all those chipped statues that were so beautiful. I'll be back, I thought as I stared up into the carved eyes of the giant sea titans holding up the entrance arch. And when I return I'll look you right in the eye and we'll see who blinks first.